The baby wasn't the only one playing havoc with her emotions, Bethany was forced to admit.

Nicholas Frakes was also having an odd effect on her equilibrium. When she first planned to interview him, she had reckoned without the sheer animal magnetism he exuded. She had never before met a man who was so…well…*male*.

On the surface he was everything she disliked in a man: physically large, which made her feel uncomfortably small and vulnerable, and so attractive that he had to be a candidate for Playboy of the Western World.

But playboys didn't usually take in orphaned babies or run themselves ragged trying to get them to eat, she acknowledged. And just being around him made her want to do reckless things…like cook and clean and take care of his baby.

Take care of *him*.

What was happening to her?

Dear Reader,

August is jam-packed with exciting promotions and top-notch authors in Silhouette Romance! Leading off the month is RITA Award-winning author Marie Ferrarella with *Suddenly...Marriage!*, a lighthearted VIRGIN BRIDES story set in sultry New Orleans. A man and woman, both determined to remain single, exchange vows in a mock ceremony during Mardi Gras, only to learn their bogus marriage is for real....

With over five million books in print, Valerie Parv returns to the Romance lineup with *Baby Wishes and Bachelor Kisses*. In this delightful BUNDLES OF JOY tale, a confirmed bachelor winds up sole guardian of his orphaned niece and must rely on the baby-charming heroine for daddy lessons—*and* lessons in love. Stella Bagwell continues her wildly successful TWINS ON THE DOORSTEP series with *The Ranger and the Widow Woman*. When a Texas Ranger discovers a stranded mother and son, he welcomes them into his home. But the pretty widow harbors secrets this lawman-in-love needs to uncover.

Carla Cassidy kicks off our second MEN! promotion with *Will You Give My Mommy a Baby?* A 911 call from a five-year-old boy lands a single mom and a true-blue, red-blooded hero in a sticky situation that quickly sets off sparks. *USA Today* bestselling author Sharon De Vita concludes her LULLABIES AND LOVE miniseries with *Baby and the Officer*. A crazy-about-kids cop discovers he's a dad, but when he goes head-to-head with his son's beautiful adoptive mother, he realizes he's fallen head over heels. And Martha Shields rounds out the month with *And Cowboy Makes Three*, the second title in her COWBOYS TO THE RESCUE series. A woman who wants a baby and a cowboy who needs an heir agree to marry but discover the honeymoon is just the beginning....

Don't miss these exciting stories by Romance's unforgettable storytellers!

Enjoy,

Joan Marlow Golan

Joan Marlow Golan
Senior Editor Silhouette Books

Please address questions and book requests to:
Silhouette Reader Service
U.S.: 3010 Walden Ave., P.O. Box 1325, Buffalo, NY 14269
Canadian: P.O. Box 609, Fort Erie, Ont. L2A 5X3

BABY WISHES AND BACHELOR KISSES

Valerie Parv

Silhouette

ROMANCE™

Published by Silhouette Books

America's Publisher of Contemporary Romance

For Lynne and Michael, in praise of all engineers

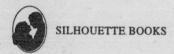 SILHOUETTE BOOKS

ISBN 0-373-19313-0

BABY WISHES AND BACHELOR KISSES

Printed in U.S.A.

Books by Valerie Parv

Silhouette Romance

The Leopard Tree #507
The Billionaire's Baby Chase #1270
Baby Wishes and Bachelor Kisses #1313

VALERIE PARV

lives and breathes romance and has even written a guide to being romantic, crediting her cartoonist husband of twenty-six years as her inspiration. As a former buffalo and crocodile hunter in Australia's Northern Territory, he's ready-made hero material, she says.

When not writing her novels and nonfiction books, or speaking about romance on Australian radio and television, Valerie enjoys dollhouses, being a Star Trek fan and playing with food (while cooking, that is). Valerie agrees with actor Nichelle Nichols, who said, "The difference between fantasy and fact is that fantasy simply hasn't happened yet."

Dear Reader,

One of my real-life heroes is Dr. Denis Waitley, a former Blue Angel and NASA advisor, now internationally acclaimed author and lecturer. In short, a man who has his act well and truly together. Yet, at his seminars he tells of being brought to his knees trying to persuade his baby daughter to eat. This delightful image provided some of the inspiration for *Baby Wishes and Bachelor Kisses,* in which hero Nicholas Frakes connects with heroine Bethany Dale as a result of a similar experience. It was probably unfair to pit him against not one but two females, one being an adorable baby girl, but I figured a man of Nicholas's caliber could handle them both.

I also wanted to explore the fascination small things hold for most of us. Whether they are human babies, baby animals or miniature objects, small things speak to all of us in a very personal way—as I notice whenever a new visitor sees my magnificent dollhouse, which holds a lifetime's collection of miniature furnishings.

It was a joy to bring so many of my passions together, resulting in one of my all-time favorite books. May it also become one of yours.

Love,

Valerie

Prologue

Nicholas Frakes drew a deep breath as his gaze rested on Maree. She was so beautiful it almost hurt to look at her, yet he felt drawn to study every detail of her over and over again as if there was a hunger inside him that her very existence was designed to satisfy.

Since moving in with him, Maree had changed his life in ways he had never imagined when he proposed the idea. Some of the changes were wonderful. He didn't have to go out in order to have female company. Maree was always there and happy to listen to him without interrupting, no matter what topic he wanted to discuss. She quite enjoyed watching sports on television, although it was obvious she didn't have a clue what was going on. But she didn't mind him explaining things in detail and generally managed to look interested.

Some of the changes were a pain in the neck. For starters, they could never agree on what time to go to bed and when to get up in the morning, so he was severely sleep-deprived from trying to adjust to her life-style. Yet she wasn't about to adjust to his, and she knew perfectly well he could deny her nothing.

She had only to look at him with those huge luminous blue eyes, and favor him with her smile, which was fit to melt stone, and he was lost. She was doing it now, regarding him curiously from under impossibly long black lashes which rested on cheeks for which the description "peaches and cream" had been invented. What was a man to do?

Then there was the matter of diet. This week she had decided to be a vegetarian, which Nicholas most certainly was not. Yet he had spent most of the morning cooking up rabbit food to keep her happy.

"Why can't you enjoy a steak like the rest of humanity?" he grumbled as he brought a dish of bland-tasting green stuff to where she waited at the table. He swore under his breath as she looked away, her expression plainly disgusted.

"Last week you couldn't get enough of this stuff," he muttered, trying to keep his temper in check. Lately they'd had more than their share of screaming matches, and he was so tired he was in no mood for another one today. What in blazes had he gotten himself into, inviting such a fickle creature into his life on a full-time basis? If he'd known what he was getting into, he would have run as far and as fast in the opposite direction as he could.

"No, I wouldn't," he contradicted himself, a smile working its way to the surface in spite of his exhaustion and ill humor. "I would still have made room for you in my life because you're my only niece. Since your mother and father were killed, you have no one else but your uncle Nicholas. And you're only ten months old, for crying out loud. No, scratch the 'crying out loud' bit. You didn't hear that, Maree. No crying, loud or otherwise. I said no crying...no...come on now, eat some of this lovely spinach."

But his pleas were drowned by the rising scale of her

wails, which lanced through his skull as if he was being attacked with a chain saw. He tried taking advantage of her open mouth to shovel some of the spinach in as a distraction, but it came out the same way, only a good deal faster.

"Maree, as much as I love you, there are times..." he growled, surveying the rivulets of pureed spinach running down his bare chest. Just as well he hadn't had time to put his shirt on this morning or he'd be changing it already. Skin was easier to launder than fabric.

Then another thought came to him, and his shaky smile broadened. Since Lana left he'd all but lost track of the days, trying to keep up with his work as an acoustical engineer, as well as take care of Maree on his own. Wasn't today the day that woman from the child care magazine was due to visit him?

Bethany Something. She had written asking if she could interview him for an article for the journal she edited called—what was it? He only knew it was something to do with babies. Lord, he could barely think straight. She must have decided to approach him as a result of a story in the local paper about what they called "the sexy single dad."

Given the circumstances under which he'd become a father, it was an insensitive approach, if it was even accurate. Single he may be, a dad definitely, but sexy? Sexy guys didn't swab spinach off their pecs, he thought ruefully as he suited the action to the thought. His brain might be fried but at least his body was still in decent shape even though he hadn't had much chance to work out since Maree moved in. She kept him as much on the run as any personal trainer.

He'd been interviewed for the last article when Maree was four months younger and sleeping most of the time, so the picture had changed since then. What Bethany What's-her-name would make of today's performance was another matter. After the insensitivity of the last write-up, he had resolved to turn any more writers away. Then it came to him that this Bethany woman might have some answers for his current problems. If so, the trade would be more than fair.

"For a start, she can tell me how to convince you to eat," he said to the screaming baby whose peaches-and-cream complexion was steadily reddening from the force of her cries. He'd tried seeking information from the local baby care authorities, but they had addressed most of their advice to his former fiancée. It was natural enough, and he didn't blame them, but it wasn't much help with Lana no longer on the scene.

Thinking of Lana provoked another sigh. As one of Australia's top fashion models and an only child to boot, she was hardly an expert on parenthood, any more than Nicholas himself. But at least he was willing to learn. Lana had said she was willing, but she had proved remarkably adept at disappearing whenever the baby was either messy or noisy, which was ninety percent of the time.

"Crying for seven hours straight last week wasn't your smartest move," he reproved the howling child gently. Lana had declared herself through with motherhood, packed her bags and left for Melbourne, to the apartment they had shared before Nicholas moved both home and consultancy back to his property in the Macedon Ranges.

Lana had hated the move and made no secret of preferring the bright-lights, big-city scene to living on a country acreage surrounded by vineyards and artists' colonies, even though he explained that a child needed growing space and room to run and play.

"How far can she run in a bassinet?" Lana had demanded.

He should have seen the end coming then, but he'd hoped that they would somehow work things out and become a family. If Lana had only waited another half hour, Maree would have cried herself to sleep.

It wouldn't have helped, he acknowledged. The baby was like a faulty fire alarm, liable to go off at any time. Like now, for instance. She was up to a three-alarm already and the decibels were still climbing. It would be easier if Maree would take to a nanny, but Nicholas would have sworn the local women he auditioned were potential ax murderers, from the way Maree reacted to them. A psychological consequence of losing her parents, he assumed.

For the first time he wondered if Lana had been jealous of the amount of time and attention Maree demanded from Nicholas. Did all babies cause such havoc in their parents' relationship? His scientist's mind worried at the question, but he was too exhausted to deal with it now. He only hoped this Bethany had some answers, because he was fresh out of them.

Chapter One

The unexpected sound of a baby screaming stopped Bethany Dale in her tracks outside the substantial colonial farmhouse that belonged to Nicholas Frakes. As far as she knew Nicholas Frakes was a bachelor. According to an old article she'd clipped from a magazine and kept, Nicholas was involved in a torrid affair with a fashion model, but there was no mention of a child. Yet the sounds coming from inside the house were unmistakable.

The front door stood open, shielded by a handsome, period-style, security screen door, and the baby's cries reached her clearly on the wide verandah that shaded the house on three sides. Bethany's reaction was instant and fierce. Waves of primitive need clawed at her, bringing a huge lump to her throat so she could hardly breathe.

Why did Nicholas Frakes have to be entertaining visitors with a baby on the day he had agreed to see Bethany? It didn't seem fair. Now she would have to conduct her interview while striving to ignore the ache she could already feel starting deep inside her.

Her eyes began to mist, and she blinked furiously. She had to get hold of herself before she rang the doorbell to announce her arrival. The world was full of babies. Just because she was unable to have any of her own was no reason to go to pieces every time she heard one crying.

Even aversion therapy hadn't helped. After discovering the truth, she had deliberately volunteered to work in the newborn room at the children's shelter in Melbourne where she worked part-time. But instead of putting her off babies, being around them had only deepened her sense of loss.

As a distraction, she had decided to throw herself into the journal she edited for people who shared her enthusiasm for dollhouses and miniatures, although the name of her publication was ironic. She had called it *The Baby House,* the name historically used to describe dollhouses before they had become children's toys. Of course, she had named it before finding out that she couldn't have children. But it was uncanny how she seemed destined to be surrounded by reminders of her barren state.

She drew a deep, shuddering breath. She was not—repeat not—going to let this beat her. Surely her parents' example was all the proof she needed that other forms of parenting could be equally gratifying? The Dale family included three foster siblings as well as Bethany, her older brother, Sam, and little sister, Joanie, and all six of them loved and fought and loved again with all the passion of blood brothers and sisters.

She could handle one unexpected baby, she told herself resolutely, especially if it meant persuading Nicholas Frakes to let her interview him about the Frakes Baby House for her journal. That was, once he got over being furious with her for concealing the real reason she was here. She hadn't lied exactly, except by omission. But she had used her business letterhead and suggested that the article would concern family history in this area. In a way, it did, she told herself to silence the nagging voice of her conscience. She hadn't said it *wasn't* about the dollhouse so she couldn't be responsible for whatever conclusions Nicholas Frakes chose to draw.

She wished she'd had more time to research his background more thoroughly but his faxed agreement, scribbled on the bottom of her letter, had come out of the blue two days before. She had been working at the children's shelter until late on both days, leaving her no time to do anything but write out a few questions she would like him to answer.

She was sure he would have refused to see her if she had mentioned the real purpose of her visit. It was Nicholas himself who had withdrawn his family's famous dollhouse from public display soon after inheriting the Frakes estate on his father's death. Why, nobody seemed to know, but he had resisted all overtures from the media to gain access to it. It would be a real coup if Bethany could secure the interview and photograph the house as it was today.

Her breath escaped in a rush. Without the boost to circulation provided by this story, her journal wouldn't survive for another issue. She could have struggled on, funding it herself, if the printer hadn't gone bankrupt while holding a substantial amount of her capital and leaving her in debt. But she couldn't let herself dwell on what was riding on this interview or she would lose her nerve altogether. And there would be no story unless she gained the cooperation of the formidable Nicholas Frakes.

Squaring her shoulders and drawing herself up to her full five foot seven, including her heeled shoes, she pressed the doorbell, hearing it ring distantly inside the house. At the same moment, the baby began to scream again louder than ever, and Bethany's heart turned over. The child sounded so desolate. Why didn't somebody do something to comfort it? In spite of her resolve to remain unmoved, her arms ached to hold the child and rock away those pathetic cries.

After the third ring, when no one came to the door, Bethany decided the occupants couldn't possibly hear her above the sound of the crying baby, so she set off around the verandah in search of another entrance where she could make her presence known.

The house was a delightful blend of traditional and modern styles, the rough-sawn timber cladding blending charmingly with bay windows, a steeply pitched corrugated roof and stained-glass panels set into French doors that could be opened onto the verandah to let in cooling breezes. One set stood open, and frothy curtains billowed outward as Bethany moved cautiously toward them.

"Hello. Is anyone home?" she called tentatively.

There was no response so she stepped over the threshold, finding herself in what was obviously a man's bedroom. A not very tidy man, she observed, wrinkling her nose involuntarily. The massive mahogany bed looked as if it hadn't been made for days, with black silk sheets and continental quilt dragging onto the floor as if the occupant had hurled himself out in a hurry.

The black silk made her smile. Definitely a bachelor. No woman in her right mind would choose such difficult-to-launder materials. Clothes were strewn everywhere, and Bethany felt her color heighten as she noticed the underwear draped over one corner of a cheval mirror. Evidently Nicholas Frakes's taste ran to skimpy briefs of almost transparent silk.

The sight of herself in the same mirror brought her up short. Her moss green linen pantsuit looked so businesslike for this setting. A black chiffon negligee would be more appropriate. No, not black—too strong for her creamy complexion, she decided. Coral was more becoming. And her honey-colored hair should be released from its clasp at her nape to flow around her shoulders in untamed curls, although the comma curl on her forehead could stay. It added a touch of coquettishness to her teal blue eyes and with luck, provided a distraction from the scattering of freckles on her fair skin. *Then* she would be ready for such a hedonistic setting as this room.

In horror she realized where her thoughts were heading. She had no right to be here, far less to be taking such a prurient interest in Nicholas Frakes's bedroom, if this was even his room. Averting her eyes from the chaos, she hurriedly crossed the room and stepped out into a wide vaulted hallway.

The crying sounds grew louder as she headed toward them. She skidded to a halt at what was apparently the door to the kitchen. It was a huge room with a massive stone fireplace and a vaulted, steeply pitched ceiling. In the center was a scarred oak table, and seated at it in a high chair was the unhappy little girl making all the noise. Beside her was an equally unhappy man trying unsuccessfully to spoon food into her mouth.

Bethany stared in amazement at the tableau. She had seen a photograph of Nicholas Frakes's head and shoulders, but it hadn't prepared her for the height and breadth of the man. A fraction over six feet tall, he stooped awkwardly over the high chair. A pair of stonewashed moleskin pants rode low on narrow hips, the seams strained to their limits as he braced his long legs wide apart. She had a momentary vision of trying to keep pace with the stride those legs would take, and she felt out of breath just thinking about it.

He wore no shirt, and his bronzed torso gleamed in the sunshine spilling through an open window, the sight putting further restraints on her breathing until she noticed the telltale green streaking the sculpted perfection of his chest. He might have the build of an athlete but he was human after all. If that wasn't spinach he was wearing, then she'd eat the baby food herself.

The discovery gave her the courage to say loudly, "Nicholas Frakes?"

The man snapped upright as if shot. "Good Lord, where did you spring from?"

She held out her hand. "I'm Bethany Dale. We had an appointment, remember? You didn't hear the bell so I came in the back way."

"The back way is locked," he said pointedly.

There was no escaping the confession, although she blushed at being forced into the admission. "The French doors into your bedroom were open. I came in that way. I'm sorry if I'm intruding."

He thrust a hand through his hair which was the blue-black color of gunmetal and cropped close to his head in almost a military style. The texture was intriguing. Would it feel soft or bristly if she brushed her fingers against it?

She was doing it again, she realized with a start. What was it about Nicholas Frakes that inspired these almost voy-euristic tendencies in her? First the underwear. Now she was wondering how it would feel to brush her fingers through his hair. And she had barely set eyes on the man.

"You're here now so the question is academic. We're almost finished. Milady is finished," he added with a tired jerk of his head toward the baby who was banging a plastic cup angrily against the tray of her high chair. "I suppose she'll eat if she gets really hungry."

Bethany glanced curiously around, putting two and two together. "You're here on your own with—"

"Maree," he supplied. "Yes, it's just me and my loud friend."

Loud was right. Bethany could hardly hear herself think over the baby's racket. She certainly couldn't conduct an interview under these conditions, even if Nicholas agreed to cooperate. For all their sakes, and especially for the sake of the little girl whose cries threatened to melt Bethany's remaining reserves, there was only one thing to do.

"Would you like some help?"

He looked so thankful as he nodded and held out the tiny spoon, that her heart was further caught in a viselike squeeze. She could see how tired he was. His bronzed skin had a pale undercast as if sleep was a distant memory, and there were violet smudges beneath both his eyes which were a compelling pewter color.

When she accepted the spoon he smiled and the fatigue cleared briefly, like a glimpse of the sun coming out on a cloudy day. The temptation to bask in the warmth of his smile was almost irresistible, and she felt her own mouth tilt upward in response. "If you can convince her to eat, I'll be forever in your debt."

She knew she wouldn't hold him to the promise, however tempting it was to turn the situation to her own advantage. Whatever cooperation she gained, he would have to give freely if she was to live with herself afterward. So she shook her head. "I'll do whatever I can to help. No obligation."

The intensity of his gaze on her was a further distraction as she dipped the spoon into the depleted bowl of pureed spinach and offered the handle of the spoon to the baby. As Bethany had hoped, Maree was so surprised by the gesture that she froze in midhowl, turning her tear-streaked face to Nicholas in confusion.

Then, hesitantly, she reached for the spoon and grasped it between chubby thumb and forefinger. Most of the spinach slid off the spoon onto the tray, and Maree watched it fall with an expression of fascination. "Ah, ah, ah," she said, then tipped the spoon so the rest of the contents joined the little pile.

Bethany pushed the bowl toward the baby. "That's it, you do it. You're a big girl, aren't you?"

She guided the hand gripping the spoon toward the food, managing to scoop some up, then helped Maree steer it toward her mouth. Nicholas's gasp of astonishment was audible between them as some of the food made it into the baby's mouth. Then with a chuckle she upended the spoon and added the rest to the pile on the tray.

"Well I'll be darned," Nicholas said in awe. "Was that what she was trying to tell me, that she wanted to feed herself?"

Bethany helped Maree to load the spoon again. "Uh-huh." She glanced at him. "She's what—nine or ten months old?"

Her sideways look caught his nod of agreement. "Ten months."

Bethany smiled. "At that age very few babies will let you feed them. They want to do it all themselves. The best solution is to give them a few soft bites of food at a time and stay out of it. They've finally worked out what their fingers are for, and they can't wait to use them at every opportunity."

He smiled back, and the tiredness lifted from his face, which positively glowed with the light of this new information. It came to her that Nicholas was a man who enjoyed learning things and wasn't too proud to let a woman teach him, provided he was sure she knew what she was talking about. The insight startled her for an instant as she became aware of a temporary bond stretching between them, forged by their concern for this adorable baby. Bethany would give a lot not to have to break that bond by revealing the real reason for her visit.

Knowing it was foolish, she couldn't bring herself to do it, at least not for the moment. She told herself it was for the baby's sake, but it wasn't the whole truth. She enjoyed the way Nicholas was looking at her, as if she was some kind of miracle worker. After her recent experience with her fiancé, Alexander Kouros, who had dumped her as soon as he discovered she couldn't have his children, it felt good to have a man look at her as if she was special and wonderful. It would change as soon as Nicholas knew why she was here, but for now it felt uncommonly good.

"You have a knack for this," he told her, his rich baritone voice admiring. "It never occurred to me that her howls were a declaration of independence."

"It wouldn't unless you know what to expect," she assured him. Working at the children's shelter, as well as helping to bring up her foster brothers and sisters, she'd had more than the usual amount of practice for her age. It made the knowledge that she could never use her experience to mother her own child all the more painful.

As she felt her eyes start to swim, she blinked furiously. She had promised herself she wasn't going to let this beat her. "There's something else we can try. Do you have any ripe bananas?"

He looked startled but moved toward the refrigerator where a well-filled fruit bowl was perched as if it had been shoved there out of harm's way. "Will this do?"

Bethany accepted the golden fruit, feeing it yield to her exploratory squeeze. "Perfect." She peeled half the fruit, broke off two small chunks and placed them in Maree's plastic bowl. "Here you go, kitten. Try these for size."

With another gurgling "ah, ah, ah" sound, the baby pincered one of the chunks and dropped it onto the pile of cold spinach. Bethany's flickering glance caught Nicholas's pained wince, but he wisely said nothing. Moments later Maree rescued the banana and poked it into her mouth, gnawing on it contentedly.

Bethany levered herself up from her kneeling position beside the high chair. "The best thing we can do is leave her to eat the banana by herself. Or not as she chooses."

"She won't choke or anything?"

She shook her head. "You don't have to leave the room. Just get on with a few chores and keep your eye on her progress, but let her make most of the running. As soon as she starts playing with the food, lift her down and wait until the next mealtime. It helps not to let her graze between meals. That way she'll be hungry for what's on the menu next time around."

"You are truly amazing. Are you sure you're real and not some kind of fairy godmother?" he asked, an appreciative light dancing in his pewter gaze. It made the years peel away so she got a momentary glimpse of the boy he must have been—handsome, devilish and irresistibly attractive. All the qualities were still there, but packaged in a body that was so undeniably male that she felt a surge of involuntary response.

What would it be like to be on the receiving end of a personal compliment from this man, she found herself wondering. She had a feeling he wouldn't bestow them idly, but neither would he withhold them if he thought they were genuinely deserved. The thought brought a flush of color to her cheeks, and she turned to watch Maree so he wouldn't see his effect on her.

Her reaction was as inappropriate as it was unexpected, and she tried to tell herself it was probably no more than a rebound thing. She had been hurt by Alexander. In his gratitude, Nicholas was being charming to her. He was also the most attractive man she'd met in a long time. It wasn't hard to see why the combination should so disturb her.

If she let it. She decided to keep the conversation on neutral ground. "All babies go through this stage. They're learning how to use their bodies and control their world, which starts with trying to control their parents. I'm sure Maree's crying has dragged her mother out in the middle of the night plenty of times lately. It's a kind of test to see if the baby can make her mother respond."

There was a long silence punctuated only by the sound of the baby playing with the banana. "I'm afraid Maree hasn't had that luxury. Her mother and father were killed seven months ago. I'm the only relative she has left."

Her gaze flew from the gurgling child to the man standing behind the high chair. He looked as if he was carved from stone but his eyes held a bleakness which tore at her. Her admiration of him soared, even as she felt her heart go out to him in his personal tragedy. "I'm so sorry. I had no idea."

"You didn't read the article in the local paper?"

She shook her head, and a frown of puzzlement etched his brow as if he had expected her to know and couldn't understand why she didn't. Was he mixing her up with another writer? The only way she could find out was by confessing her real purpose and now didn't seem like the right time. "I'm afraid not. If you'd rather I went away and came back some other time." She was gathering up her bag as she spoke.

His hand on her arm stayed her. "You don't have to leave. It still hurts to think about, but I've had time to come to terms with what happened."

The heat of his touch sent awareness flashing through her, as incandescent as a signal flare. Her eyes widened. Had Nicholas felt it, too? With an effort she met his eyes and made herself ask, "Was it an accident?"

He nodded. "There was a signal failure at a railway crossing not far from here. My brother and sister-in-law were driving across when an express train slammed into their car without any warning. Maree was the only survivor because she was strapped into a baby seat. Even then, given the state of the car, it was a miracle she survived. There wasn't a scratch on her."

This time when her eyes blurred she made no attempt to conceal it from him. "What a terrible tragedy."

"It was, but all we can do is go on."

"As you're doing with your little niece?"

He nodded. "I'm all she has in the world, and I mean to give her the best upbringing I possibly can."

The baby, her cheeks bulging with bananas, looked the picture of health and happiness as she bounced up and down in her high chair. Apart from the recent adornment of pureed spinach, she was spotlessly clean, dressed in a gorgeous romper suit decorated in teddy bears, with a pink ribbon adorning one of her baby curls.

She was in far better condition than her uncle, Bethany decided. Nicholas looked as if he had thrown his pants on in haste and forgotten—or never had time—to shave this morning. A bluish tinge darkened the strong line of his jaw, giving him a rugged, almost-piratical appearance which was more appealing than it had any right to be. The fatigue darkening his eyes only added to his masculine appeal, and to her horror, Bethany found herself wishing she could do something to help.

This would never do. She was here for one purpose and one only, to persuade him to let her write about the Frakes Baby House. But how could she come out and say so now, when he had just revealed the depths of a personal tragedy far greater than she had anticipated?

She couldn't, she decided. Her hand closed resolutely around her bag. "I should go. The interview can wait until another time."

"Dammit, you needn't start feeling sorry for me," he growled, startling her into freezing where she stood. "I've had enough of that from my neighbors around here. They act as if Maree and I have a contagious disease called tragedy. When you walked in knowing nothing about out situation, you treated us just like anybody else and it was like a breath of fresh air. At least stay and have a cup of coffee with me. You said yourself the best thing to do is keep busy in the kitchen while Maree feeds herself.''

Bethany gave a wan smile. "All right, one cup of coffee. But only if it's no trouble.''

"After the morning I've had, coffee isn't any trouble, it's a medical necessity,'' he assured her. "How do you take yours?''

"Black with one sugar,'' she supplied, settling herself on a high stool next to a breakfast counter. It was cluttered with the remains of what looked like his breakfast, and she smiled wryly at the sight of an open packet of chocolate-flavored cereal, a milk carton and a plastic bowl, the twin of the one Maree was using. Evidently Nicholas didn't believe in healthy breakfasts, for himself, anyway.

As he spooned coffee into the pot, he looked up in time to catch her smile. "What?''

"No wonder you look so tired if you're existing on this stuff,'' she observed.

He shrugged. "Who has time to cook?''

She surprised herself by saying, "If you keep an eye on the baby, I'll make you an omelette that will make your mouth water.''

His mouth looked as if it was watering at the very idea. His sweeping gesture took in the refrigerator and stove. "Be my guest. Everything you're likely to need is here.''

He moved aside to let her take over the food preparation area, and she surveyed the gleaming modern stove with apprehension. She must be crazy letting a misguided sense of compassion drive her to volunteer for this. Or was she simply delaying the moment when she had to disillusion him by admitting why she was really here?

Whatever the reason, it was too late to back out now. Nicholas had thrown himself into a comfortable-looking oversize leather chair which flanked the stone fireplace. He watched with interest as she whipped up eggs and milk, shredded cheese and added a few leaves of parsley from a pot growing on the windowsill, then set the mixture sizzling in a large cast-iron pan.

It did smell good, she thought with a flush of pride, as she placed a plate on a small table beside him a few minutes later. He eyed the golden creation hungrily. "You really are a miracle worker if you cook as well as you charm babies."

A perverse streak of pride prevented her from admitting that an omelette was the only thing she could cook, other than baby food. Her brother Sam called her the "Thrill Griller" because he never knew what was going to come out of her culinary efforts. More often than not it was a charred mess. In defiance, to avoid being the butt of any more family jokes whenever it was her turn to cook dinner, she had gritted her teeth and mastered the art of making omelettes. Served with a salad, her cheese omelette could pass any test.

It was doing so now, she saw as Nicholas proceeded to demolish the six egg treat with total disdain for the risk to his arteries from all that cholesterol. She had loaded the omelette with extra cheese since he looked as if he could use the fuel. "This is good," he mumbled around a forkful of food. He sounded so much like Maree with her banana that Bethany had to smother a laugh. She didn't think he would appreciate the comparison.

To distract herself while he ate, she tidied up the remains of the baby's meal then draped a towel over her shoulder and lifted Maree out of the high chair, resting her against the towel. Several hearty burps later, one of which she would swear hadn't come from the baby, Bethany handed Maree to her surrogate father. "Both of you look disgustingly satisfied," she observed, feeing an unwilling frisson of pleasure at her own part in the achievement.

Nicholas began to jiggle Maree on his knee, and the baby

chortled happily. "I'd say we're both in luck with our fairy godmother, don't you agree, Mareedle-deedle-dumpling?" The baby gurgled what sounded like agreement. "There, you see? The expert in fairy godmothers agrees with me."

Bethany felt an ache so sharp and fierce that at first she didn't connect it with the sight of the big man cradling the baby against the hard wall of his bare chest. But nothing else could explain the intensity of the pain which knifed through her. It had to be the image of Maree's dark head nestled in the angle between Nicholas's powerful jaw and his chest. He rested one hand lightly against Maree's back while the other cupped her chubby hips as if holding a baby was the most natural thing in the world to him.

Bethany was gripped by a need so powerful it threatened her breathing. She turned away and forced herself to say around a betraying huskiness, "I'll finish making the coffee."

The simple act of locating cups and pouring the brewed coffee into them helped to anchor her so that by the time she turned to ask Nicholas how he preferred his coffee, her hands no longer trembled.

She needn't have worried. In the few minutes it took her to pour the coffee, both Nicholas and the baby resting on his chest were fast asleep.

Chapter Two

"Oh my." Bethany finally allowed her eyes to brim as she sagged against the breakfast counter. Nothing was going to disturb Nicholas and Maree for a while. They made such a heartwarming sight that she would have felt moved to tears even without the biological need clamoring at her.

The baby wasn't the only one playing havoc with her emotions, Bethany was forced to admit as she sipped the coffee moodily. Nicholas Frakes was also having an odd effect on her equilibrium. When she first planned to interview him, she had reckoned without the sheer animal magnetism he exuded. She had never before met a man who was so...well...*male*.

On the surface he was everything she disliked in a man: physically large, which made her feel uncomfortably small and vulnerable; messy and disorganized, when she preferred everything to be in its place; and so attractive that he had to be a candidate for Playboy of the Western World.

All right, she was clutching at straws with this last one. Playboys didn't usually take in orphaned babies or run

themselves ragged trying to get them to eat, she acknowledged, her innate sense of fair play springing to the fore.
He did have *some* redeeming qualities. But he was still
large and messy, and just being around him made her want
to do reckless things like cook and clean and take care of
his baby.

What was going on here?

She gave herself a mental shake. Finding Nicholas in
charge of a baby when it was the last thing she'd expected
must be distorting her perception. It was also making her
forget that she was here under false pretenses. Nicholas
believed *The Baby House* had something to do with child
care. Once he knew her journal was for dollhouse enthusiasts, it would be the end of her fairy godmother image.
He probably wouldn't be able to get her out of his house
fast enough.

The thought was enough to banish the mistiness from
her eyes. She finished the coffee and looked around. Inter-
viewing Nicholas was out of the question until he'd slept
off his exhaustion, so she may as well make herself useful.
It might even weigh in her favor when he was deciding
whether or not to throw her out on her ear.

She started in the kitchen, collecting and washing the
accumulated dishes and sweeping the floor. Searching
around for a garbage bin, she almost fell over two baskets
of clothes waiting to be washed in the laundry. She gave a
sigh. In for a penny…

Luckily the laundry was well organized, so she soon had
the clothes sorted and the first load humming away in the
modern machine. There was enough here for three loads,
she thought, stooping to sort the remaining basket. Didn't
Nicholas believe in doing laundry? Or was he waiting for
his live-in lady friend to return and do it for him?

Maybe she was the driving force behind providing a
home for Maree, Bethany thought with sudden insight.

Bethany had given Nicholas all the credit, but maybe it belonged to the missing model she'd read about in the outdated magazine.

As if to prove her theory, Bethany came across a silk blouse at the bottom of the last basket. It definitely didn't belong to Nicholas, and Maree was too young for such delicate apparel. That left the model who was probably away on a photographic assignment. Bethany swore under her breath at her own gullibility. If she'd used her head in the first place, she would have realized that no man slept on black satin sheets for his own amusement.

She had only herself to blame. Just as she had avoided telling Nicholas the real reason for her visit, he hadn't actually *said* he lived alone with the baby, only that he was on his own today. So they were even in the lying-by-omission stakes. Somehow the thought was little comfort, and Bethany finished sorting the laundry with angry movements, slamming the washing machine lid down harder than was warranted. She wasn't entirely sure why she was so angry, except that she was.

A wave of guilt washed over her as she heard a chorus of wails from the kitchen. By making such a racket all she'd managed to do was wake the baby. It didn't bode well for the rest of the afternoon.

Nicholas didn't look angry when he tracked her down in the laundry. He looked bemused at all she'd achieved while he slept. "You should have woken me. I should be doing that," he told her, folding his arms and angling his body comfortably against the door frame.

She forced herself to ignore the impact of his presence in the small room. "Is Maree all right?"

"Rested, changed and playing with her toys in her playpen," he informed her with a grin. "Changing her is one job I do know how to get right, maybe because I get so much practice at it."

In spite of herself she felt a glow steal through her at the warmth of his smile, which was slightly crooked and showed the even whiteness of his teeth. The difference in their heights put her eyes close to the level of his mouth. A very kissable mouth, she found herself thinking. A mouth that could give as well as command. Another wave of heat curled through her, this time unmistakably sensual, and she ran her tongue across suddenly dry lips. This would have to stop since no good could come of it. Nicholas was already spoken for. She had the evidence right here in her hands.

She held out the filmy white blouse. "I didn't think this should go in with the other clothes. It's obviously delicate. When your friend comes home, she may prefer to have it dry-cleaned."

A shadow darkened his features. "Lana's unlikely to care either way. Country life didn't suit her. She went home to Melbourne and she isn't coming back."

Bethany let the blouse fall back into the basket. "I'm sorry." She was making a habit of apologizing to him, but this time she didn't feel in the least sorry. She felt curiously elated to discover that the mysterious Lana had left, apparently for good. It was hardly a charitable response but she couldn't seem to stop herself.

"These things happen," he said dismissively, but the tension in his neck and shoulders wasn't lost on her. He cared more than he wanted to admit. Well it was none of her business. She had already entangled herself in his domestic affairs far more than was wise. She had come here to do a job, not to get involved in his private life.

All the same it was difficult to respond with a casual nod, when she knew firsthand how painful it felt to be left nursing a wounded heart. "Shouldn't you look in on Maree?" she made herself ask pointedly.

His piercing gaze rested on her for a long moment before

he said, "Of course. You can leave the rest of the laundry for me. You've done more than enough already. I don't know how I can possibly repay you."

This was the opening she'd waited for, but she balked at taking advantage of it. "I'll be happy with the interview I requested," she said lightly, knowing she should use this chance to persuade him to give her the story. She couldn't do it, she found to her dismay. If this was to work, he had to agree of his own volition. She couldn't bring herself to blackmail him into it in exchange for the few chores she'd undertaken of her own accord.

He gave another crooked grin and held out his hand to help her step over the laundry baskets. "I could finish this," she said with a backward look at the clothes, but his grip tightened and he towed her into the kitchen where Maree played happily in her playpen.

"Are you always this helpful to your interview subjects?" he asked, a lilt of wry humor in his tone. "If I'd known, you could have arrived earlier and worked your way through the rest of the housework."

Thinking of the state of the bedroom she'd walked through on her way in, she shook her head. "No thanks. My life isn't long enough."

He pretended to be offended. "My housekeeping isn't *that* bad. All right, maybe it is. But I have a consultancy to run as well as taking care of Maree. Editing a baby care magazine, you of all people should know how much time a toddler takes up."

His hand in hers was warm, his strong fingers curling into her palm as if he had forgotten to release her now they were back in the kitchen. Slowly, aware of a feeling of reluctance, she untangled her hand. "Nicholas, we have to talk. I know my journal is called *The Baby House* but it isn't what you think."

"It isn't about babies?"

"Not really." She took a steadying breath. The truth had to come out sometime, and she had already postponed it far longer than was wise. "*The Baby House* is a specialized journal for collectors of miniatures and...dollhouses."

The slow burn of his anger was evident from the rigidity of his stance and the way his hands curled into fists at his sides. "Dollhouses?"

Miserably, she nodded. "They were known as baby houses in Victorian times when furniture makers and decorators used them to show off their skills, and women displayed collections of valuable miniatures in them, long before they became children's toys."

"Now I understand why you didn't know about Maree from the story in the local paper," he said coldly. "This isn't about her, or about any kind of family history, is it?"

Bethany's look went to the baby playing with a set of brightly colored plastic cups, oblivious of the storm breaking around her. "In a way, what I want to write does concern your family history. I want to do a story about the Frakes Baby House."

His breath escaped in a whistling sound of annoyance. "If you know about that, then you must know I'm not interested in having it on public show. So your little scheme to get around me by pretending to be something you're not was a waste of time."

She had been prepared for the switch from friendliness to hostility as soon as he found out what she wanted, but his callous attack on her integrity made her see red. She didn't stop to consider whether she would be less angry if he hadn't charmed her so completely to begin with. "Now just a minute. I wrote to you on my business letterhead, asking for an interview. You were the one who jumped to the wrong conclusions."

"And it never crossed your mind that I would?"

"Of course it did. But I hoped once we met and I explained to you what I wanted, you would see reason."

He crossed his arms, towering over her in a blatant invasion of her space. "So you think it's unreasonable of me to want to maintain my privacy?"

She stood her ground, determined not to back away and reveal how disturbing she found his closeness. "I don't think it's unreasonable at all. But my story doesn't have to be an invasion of your privacy. If you don't want me to, I won't even mention your name."

His eyes glittered ferally. "You'll just refer to it as the Brand X Baby House?"

She couldn't and he knew it. All she could do was retreat as gracefully as possible. She only wished it didn't hurt so much. He hadn't even given her a chance to explain what she wanted to do, and she still had no idea why he hated the idea of giving any publicity to the dollhouse that had been in his family for generations.

Nor did she understand why it mattered so much to her—not the story, although without it she had almost no chance of saving her journal—but why his good opinion was so important to her that it hurt to be on the receiving end of his derision. She had enjoyed being called a miracle worker and a fairy godmother, but there was more. She had enjoyed the appreciative way he looked at her, even the enthusiasm with which he ate the one thing she cooked well.

Pity help her, she had even enjoyed doing his cleaning and laundry.

For a couple of hours she had felt like a normal, functioning woman, she realized with a heavy heart. After the way Alexander had dumped her because she couldn't have his children, it had felt good to be appreciated by a man, even one who didn't really know her. In the guise of helping Nicholas out, she had been playing house, and now it had to stop.

"Thanks for your time. I'll see myself out," she said, picking up her bag. This time he didn't try to stop her, and she was thankful the security door opened easily from the inside. She didn't fancy having to retrace her steps past the kitchen and out through his bedroom. As she made her way slowly back to her car, which was parked in the shade of a golden wattle tree, she heard Maree start to cry. Bethany's footsteps faltered but she made herself keep walking.

"Women. You can't trust 'em as far as you can throw 'em," Nicholas seethed, hearing the sound of the security door swing shut. He aimed a kick at a cupboard door and winced as the pain jarred all the way up his leg. "Damn. I should have known she was up to something. Baby house, indeed. She probably thought all she had to do was cook a meal and wash my laundry, and I'd be putty in her hands. Well it didn't work, did it, Maree? We told her where to get off, didn't we?"

Hearing her name, the baby looked up, but at the sight of his furious expression, she screwed up her face and dissolved into tears and started banging a plastic cup disconsolately against the bars of her playpen, the sound keeping time with her wails.

Despair coiled through Nicholas. Now look what the wretched woman had done, he thought. She'd managed to upset the baby, just when he'd gotten her quiet and happy. He leaned over the side of the pen, reaching for the child. "Come here, little darling. Don't cry. I'm not mad at you. I'm mad at Bethany."

At the sound of the name, Maree's tear-filled eyes widened and she began to beat at Nicholas's chest. "Ah, ah, ah," she screamed, punctuating the sounds with blows.

He regarded the baby curiously. "Bethany? You're telling me you like Bethany?"

Every time he said the name, there was a fresh gurgle of "ah, ah, ah" sounds.

He shook his head. "Trust me, we're better off without her. Just because she happens to be damnably attractive—" He broke off as Bethany's image filled his mind. She *was* attractive, he realized. He couldn't recall seeing hair that exact shade of gold before, as if it was perpetually in sunlight. She had nice eyes, too, now he came to think about it. They reminded him of the sky on a summer day. Odd that all the comparisons he could think of related to sunshine.

Her voice was unusual, too, faintly musical and pitched in the lower register, which appealed to his trained ear. When she laughed he could hear wind chimes. He wouldn't mind recording and analyzing her voice. He was willing to bet even the wavelengths would be picturesque.

"Not that I have any such intentions," he told Maree severely, annoyed with himself for letting his thoughts run away with him. "The woman's devious and manipulative. All her schmoozing with you was to get around me. She probably doesn't even like babies."

Even as he said it he knew it wasn't true. All he had to do was compare Bethany's behavior toward Maree with Lana's. They were like chalk and cheese. Anything Lana did for Maree was on sufferance and she didn't care who knew it. If she could have held the child at arm's length like a piece of soiled clothing she would have done so. Bethany had shown no such aversion, even pitching in to do the laundry without a second thought.

Why hadn't she simply told him what she wanted instead of sneaking around pretending to be a child care expert?

Because she was right—if she was honest she wouldn't have gotten to first base with him because of his stupid hang-up about that blasted dollhouse. She couldn't know why he was so averse to letting the thing see the light of day, and he was in no hurry to explain himself to her. It was probably foolish, but a man had a right to his own kinds of foolishness.

What he didn't have a right to do was treat her as badly as he had. "You're right," he said to the baby in his arms. "What you and I have to do is apologize to Bethany for the way we acted. It's the least we can do before she leaves."

The baby bounced up and down in his grasp, grabbing and pulling at strands of his hair. "Ah, ah, ah."

He gave a yelp of pain but got her message. "Okay, *I* have to apologize. You got along with her like a house on fire. Come on then, let's go eat humble pie. But I should warn you, it tastes worse than pureed spinach."

Bethany was fumbling in her bag for her car keys when the crunch of footsteps on the gravel surface of the driveway made her look up. Nicholas came toward her carrying Maree in his arms, and the baby's face lit up at the sight of her new friend.

Bethany tried to harden her heart with little success. It was small consolation that she had won a convert in the Frakes family, when it wasn't the one who could help her. She lifted her head and met Nicholas's eyes with a defiance she was far from feeling. "Was there another insult you forgot to throw at me?"

He cleared his throat. "What I forgot, and this little lady reminded me, was simple human courtesy. Is it too late to say I'm sorry for acting so hotheaded?"

It was so unexpected that she was momentarily at a loss for words, which her siblings would have found amusing in the extreme. What she lacked in cooking ability she usually made up for in conversational skills. When she finally found her voice she felt bound to be honest. "I deserved some of what you said. You were right, I should have told you what I wanted from the beginning.''

"You probably should, but it doesn't justify my biting your head off, even if I was tired to the bone.''

Against her better judgment Bethany responded to the sincerity in his tone and smiled back. "I know what it's like. Considering how small they are, babies demand enormous amounts of time, attention and love. I can hardly criticize you for giving them to Maree.''

He frowned. "If this *Baby House* of yours isn't about baby care, how come you know so much about them?''

"I have five brothers and sisters, four of them much younger than me, so I got a lot of practice at helping to bring them up. I'm also a casual worker at a shelter for disadvantaged children in Melbourne.''

He nodded as if she had confirmed something for him. Then he nuzzled the baby's tiny pink ear. "You know, Maree, you are wise for one so young." She gurgled a response and he pretended to listen with rapt attention before nodding again. "Good idea, little darling. Exactly what I was thinking myself.''

Baffled, Bethany observed the strange, one-sided conversation, bemused by the way Maree seemed to understand everything Nicholas was saying. Which was more than Bethany herself did. "Excuse me?''

"Oh, sorry. I was consulting my friend here about an idea we just had. Do you know you're the first person besides me that Maree has taken to since her parents died?''

What about the lovely Lana, Bethany couldn't help wondering, but decided to quit while she was ahead. Leaving on good terms with him had seemed impossible a few moments ago. She should be thankful for small mercies.

As if to prove his point, the baby leaned out of Nicholas's embrace and stretched out her arms toward Bethany. "Ah, ah, ah.''

Bethany reacted instinctively, setting her bag on the roof of the car and reaching to take the child from Nicholas. "See what I mean?" he said as the baby wrapped her arms around Bethany's neck.

The child smelled sweetly of milk and baby powder, and Bethany buried her face in the satiny folds of her neck, making trilling noises with her lips and tongue. The vibrations made Maree chuckle and the sound resonated through Bethany like music. How could anyone not take to such a delightful little creature? Gradually she became aware of Nicholas watching her with something very much like satisfaction. What was going on here?

Since he didn't seem to be in any hurry to enlighten her, she gave Maree one last hug and forced herself to hand the child back, closing her ears to the chorus of protesting noises. "I'd better be on my way. Thanks for clearing the air." She tickled Maree under the chin. "Goodbye little one. It was fun meeting you."

"You don't have to leave," Nicholas startled her by saying.

Was he going to grant her the interview after all? She forced down a sudden rush of excitement. If he had changed his mind, it must be for his own reasons. Until she knew what they were, it was as well not to get her hopes up. She might not be willing to meet his terms.

"I don't?" she echoed, knowing she sounded foolish but unable to think of a more profound response. Where was the outgoing, articulate Bethany Dale now? Tongue-tied by the nearness of a man she didn't like, who certainly didn't like her, but who could make her feel hot and breathless simply by standing within two feet of her.

Nicholas gave her a level look while Maree played with his hair. "If you still want that story, maybe we can work something out."

A sinking feeling gripped her. Surely Nicholas Frakes

wasn't going to turn out to be one of those men who reduced everything to sexual favors?

She drew herself up, uncomfortably aware that she was trapped between her car and Nicholas's hard body. But he was hampered by the baby in his arms. "I'm afraid I don't need the interview that much," she snapped.

For a half second he looked puzzled, then angry as light dawned. "Good grief, woman, this has nothing to do with your body. Just because Lana's gone doesn't mean I'm desperate yet."

Contrarily, rather than reassuring her, his comment hurt more than she could believe possible. "Well thank you very much."

Evidently realizing his mistake, he tried again. "I don't mean I'd have to be desperate to be interested in you. You're a beautiful woman, and from what I've seen today, you're going to make some man incredibly happy. But this has nothing to do with you and me," he insisted. "I want you to help me take care of Maree."

This last came out in such a roar that the baby looked startled. It was nothing compared to the way Bethany felt. She had practically accused him of harassment when all he wanted was her parenting skills. He also thought she was beautiful, she couldn't help noticing, and resisted examining how *that* felt. "You want me as a baby-sitter?" she asked, dumbfounded.

"In return for conditional access to the Frakes Baby House," he confirmed. He raked one hand through his close-cropped hair. "What on earth did you think I was going to propose?"

If she hadn't been so aware of him as a man, she probably wouldn't have jumped to stupid conclusions, she told herself, wondering at the same time if there wasn't an element of wishful thinking there, too. Did she want him to

want her? Even though her mind produced an instant denial
she suspected she wasn't being entirely honest with herself.

"I don't know what I was thinking. It's been a confusing
day," she dissembled. "One minute you can't wait to get
rid of me and the next you want to hire me on a daily
basis."

"Not daily, full-time, live-in, although I'm glad I didn't
suggest it right off the bat, or goodness knows what conclusions you'd have drawn."

"There's no need to rub it in," she said, feeling her face
flame. In case she still harbored doubts, he was emphasiz-
ing that he wasn't interested in her as a woman, but purely
as a potential caretaker for Maree. The thought stung, but
she had only herself to blame for misinterpreting his first
overture.

He watched her closely. "Interested?"

"I don't know about living in," she said. Most of her
misgivings stemmed from her own reactions to Nicholas
himself. He might not be interested in her, but she couldn't
deny the flaring of attraction she felt around him. Sharing
close quarters with him amounted to playing with fire, and
she'd already been burned by her relationship with Alexander. She didn't need another lesson in her inadequacies
as a woman.

Not that she'd get it from Nicholas. Was that what she
really feared, that she could live under his roof without
affecting him in the slightest, while he had the opposite
effect on her?

"Before the accident, my brother and sister-in-law lived
here and had set the place up as bed-and-breakfast accommodation. So, you would have your own self-contained
quarters," he went on. "You'd have to live in because it's
too far to commute from Melbourne every day. Besides
which, my work involves clients all over the world, so I'm
at the computer till all hours. With you here, I might finally

manage to catch up on some sleep. As well as giving you access to the dollhouse, I'm prepared to pay well for your services."

The salary he named would get her out of financial trouble for some time to come. Added to the appeal of a story about the long-lost Frakes Baby House, the package would enable her to clear her debts and bring her business back from the brink.

"It's only until I can find someone to fill the job permanently," he added when she hesitated. "Surely the children's shelter can spare you for a time?"

"As a casual, I work whatever shifts I'm available, so leave isn't the problem."

"Then what is the problem?"

He was, she admitted inwardly. No man had ever excited her the way Nicholas did. From the moment she set eyes on him, her response had been instant and annoyingly physical. If she agreed to work for him would it get worse, or would familiarity end up breeding contempt? There was only one way to find out.

"Your offer does have its attractions," she said with more irony than he could possibly know, "but we need to get a few things straight. First, I'd love to look after Maree but I'm not a housekeeper."

"Not a problem," he confirmed. "I'll get someone to clean the house and take care of the laundry."

"And I'm a terrible cook," she confessed in a rush.

"But your omelette was the best I've ever tasted."

"It's the only thing of mine you'll ever taste. In fact it's the only thing I can cook. So if that disqualifies me for the job..."

"No, no," he denied hastily. "Maree is my first concern and you have her approval, which is what matters. As it happens I'm a passable cook when I'm not so worn out, so we can alternate my dinners with your omelettes. Do we have a deal?"

It was probably the craziest thing she had ever done, but she found herself nodding. "We have a deal."

Chapter Three

Sam Dale loaded another box into Bethany's hatchback. "Are you sure you have enough stuff in here? I can tie the refrigerator to the back if you like."

Bethany pulled a face at him. "Very funny. It only looks like a lot because it's a small car. I didn't pack too much because I'll only be at Yarrawong until Nicholas Frakes finds someone compatible to take care of Maree permanently."

"Compatible with whom?"

To her annoyance Bethany felt herself redden. "With the baby, of course. He isn't the slightest bit interested in me, only in how well I get along with Maree." How could he be interested in Bethany after being involved with a famous beauty like Lana Sinden?

Sam's eyes narrowed. "Are you sure he isn't interested in you? Forgive my suspicious mind, and I'll probably hate myself for admitting this, but you *are* an attractive female, even if you are my little sister. I don't like the idea of you moving in with a virtual stranger."

"I'm going to work for him, not move in with him, as you put it," Bethany denied. Her brother's compliment, instead of his usual merciless teasing, was a measure of his concern for her. She draped an arm around his shoulders, although she had to reach up a good eight inches to do so. "Relax, big brother. In the first place, twenty-five isn't so little anymore. And in the second, when I called his professional organization, they acted as if I wanted a reference for God."

Sam whirled her off her feet, then set her down again. "At least I've taught you some sense over the years. What does this guy do, anyway?"

She frowned, recalling what she had learned. "This guy as you call him is Dr. Nicholas Frakes, Ph.D., and he does consulting work in acoustical engineering for the government. I gather most of his work is classified, but it has something to do with measures to counteract military and industrial eavesdropping."

Sam grinned. "So walls really do have ears these days?"

"So it seems. All you have to do is point the right laser gadget at a building to hear everything that's going on inside."

"Maybe I should hire one and park myself outside your new boss's property."

She threw a beach towel at him. "Go wash your mind out with soap."

Sam's grin widened as he snatched the towel out of midair. "You're attracted to the good doctor, aren't you?"

"Of course not." The denial sounded forced even to her own ears.

"Then why are you going to work for him. If it's only the money there are lots of jobs you can do right here in Melbourne, without marooning yourself in the hills."

Bethany had asked herself the same question many times in the few days since she accepted Nicholas's proposition.

Sam didn't know how desperate she was for money right now, and she had no intention of telling him. He would bankrupt himself before letting her struggle, which was precisely why he couldn't know the full extent of her problems. His fledgling furniture-making business was far from prosperous, and although she had no doubt it would be one day, for now he needed every cent of his capital to keep his own business afloat.

He was right, it wasn't only money that attracted her to working for Nicholas Frakes. The salary he had offered would solve a lot of her problems, and being able to write about the Frakes Baby House was also a coup, but it still didn't explain why she felt such a strong need to accept the job.

In Nicholas's kitchen she had experienced a real sense of belonging, of being accepted without judgment—something her recent experience with Alexander Kouros had made her wonder if she would ever know again. She had been so sure she and Alexander had had a future, although now that she thought about it, his voluble, multigeneration family had always overwhelmed her a little. She was used to large families, but the sense of tradition pervading the Kouros household was stronger than anything in her own family.

Among the Dales, people were accepted on their own merits, innocent until proven guilty and even then cut a considerable amount of slack. Alexander's father ruled his family with an iron hand, making it clear that Alexander, as the oldest son, would carry on the family's catering business and most important of all, the family name.

In front of everyone, Stavros and Ellie, Alexander's father and mother, had happily discussed their future daughter-in-law's breeding potential. Bethany's full hips, a source of annoyance to her for years, had pleased them as a sign that she could bear many strong, healthy sons.

It had never occurred to any of them that her hips were the only part of her suited to childbearing. Unknown to anyone including Bethany herself until she needed a checkup for a minor complaint, her ability to have children had been destroyed by the aftereffects of a ruptured appendix in her teens.

She had expected Alexander to be as devastated as she was, but she had also expected his love and support. When he learned that surgery offered her a less than thirty percent chance of removing the scar tissue, he had urged her to go ahead although she explained that the operation couldn't guarantee she would ever be able to conceive.

She would never forget his disgusted expression when she had suggested fostering or adopting children as her own parents had done.

"They would not have Kouros blood," he had said, unconsciously echoing his father's arrogant tones. "It is not a viable alternative." Then he had walked out.

She had accepted that it was over but hadn't expected it to hurt so much. Finding out she would never have a baby of her own was bad enough, but Alexander's rejection had made her feel like damaged goods. The pain still dragged at her, and she knew that her motive to accept Nicholas's offer was as much for the chance to remind herself of all she still had to offer as it was to solve her financial worries.

Her reverie was interrupted by a shrill call from Bethany's first-floor window. It was Amanda, Sam's current girlfriend, who'd come along supposedly to help with the packing, but had spent most of the time drinking coffee and looking decorative. "Telephone for you, Beth. It's Nick Frakes."

Bethany gritted her teeth. "Coming." To Sam, she said, "Can't you convince *Mandy* that I hate being called Beth?" She enjoyed it about as much as she imagined Nicholas would like being referred to as Nick.

Sam shrugged. "I've told her but she forgets."

"What does she call you?"

"What do you think? Samuel, of course."

Maybe Nicholas had changed his mind about hiring her, Bethany thought as she took the stairs two at a time. Maybe Lana Sinden had returned and decided three would be a crowd. It was a surprisingly depressing idea. Bethany silenced the fruitless speculation with a frown. She would know the answer in another two seconds.

Amanda was waiting by the phone and didn't move away when Bethany picked up the receiver. Cursing her brother's taste in women, she turned her back slightly. "Hello, Nicholas?"

"Bethany, thank goodness. Maree's been giving me a hard time ever since you left. I think it's her way of letting me know she wants you back. How soon can you get here?"

Something caught deep in Bethany's chest, and she pressed a hand between her breasts as if to calm the sudden leaping of her heart. Knowing he was only concerned because of the baby couldn't dampen her instinctive excitement at hearing his voice.

The breath she took to steady herself wasn't nearly sufficient. "We agreed I'd arrive tomorrow afternoon, but I'm all packed. I can drive up this afternoon if you like." Now who sounded overeager?

"Bless you, that would be great. What time...excuse me a moment."

He broke off to speak to someone in the background, and Bethany felt her smile turn brittle. The voice in the background was unmistakably female. Bethany couldn't make out the words, but the woman's musical laughter was answered by Nicholas's honeyed tones. No wonder he wanted Bethany there as soon as possible. It sounded as if Maree was getting in the way of his reunion with Lana

Sinden. Maree had come between them once before. He was probably ensuring it didn't happen again.

When he came back to the phone she said stiffly, "I can be there by five."

He didn't seem to notice her change of tone. "Terrific. We'll have your room ready."

The plural wasn't lost on her as she slowly replaced the receiver. Nor was the awareness that some of the pleasure had just gone out of the day.

The feeling dimmed some of her appreciation of the drive north from Melbourne along the Calder Freeway toward the Macedon Ranges. Only as the ranges began to lose their purple haze and turn into the famed "hills of gold" where fortunes had been made and lost during the gold rushes of the previous century did she start to relax. In accepting this job she wasn't looking for the "gold" of a relationship so what did it matter if Nicholas Frakes and Lana Sinden had kissed and made up? Maree was the only one who mattered.

She smiled as she thought of the baby. In spite of the tragedy in her short life the child had a delightfully outgoing personality, a far cry from some of the disadvantaged babies who passed through the children's shelter in Melbourne—some battered, others neglected, and all so hungry for love and attention that sometimes Bethany could hardly bear it. As a result of their experiences, many of them were afraid to trust themselves to give and receive love.

Bethany's hands tightened around the steering wheel. If she wasn't careful she would end up like those babies, too emotionally bruised to trust in her own lovability. Then she would be as much to blame as Alexander for allowing it to happen.

"No," she said aloud, startling herself. Maybe Nicholas Frakes wasn't for her, but he wasn't the only man in the world. Neither was Alexander. Out there somewhere was a man she could love with all her heart and who would cherish her for her own sake, not for what she could or couldn't give him.

Angry at allowing herself to doubt it for a minute, she blinked away the mist that clouded her eyes in time to spot the round tower of Australia's only surviving bluestone windmill. Standing by the Metcalfe Road just beyond the town of Kyneton, it marked the turnoff which led to an old coach road and onto the Frakes estate of Yarrawong.

Set in fourteen acres of land with its own mineral springs and stands of tall timber, Yarrawong lay at the heart of bluestone country, characterized by stone bridges and viaducts, mills and colonial cottages. Surrounded by the ranges and forests of the spectacular Central Highlands it had been a favorite haunt of bushrangers but now offered a haven of peace and quiet, exactly what she needed right now. If only Lana Sinden was as happy as Nicholas to have Bethany here, came the reluctant afterthought.

Well, she was about to find out.

Turning in at the open wrought iron gates leading to the homestead, she drove along a tree-lined avenue to the house, which was set among magnificent red gums, a huge Moreton Bay fig and graceful peppertrees. Despite her apprehension over what sort of welcome she could expect, a feeling of well-being crept over her and she started to hum under her breath.

This time her arrival was not greeted by earsplitting screams. Almost before the peals of the doorbell died away, Nicholas appeared at the front door, Maree in his arms. Bethany drew in a sharp breath. She had told herself she wouldn't be affected by the sight of him, but her body had other ideas.

In contrast to her last visit, today he looked not only rested but freshly overhauled, dressed casually but impeccably in dark slacks and a butter-colored polo shirt, open at the neck. The strong line of his jaw was emphasized by a thorough shave. The faint scent of his aftershave lotion teased at her nostrils, the spicy fragrance mingling with his own distinctive man smell to make a heady blend.

"Come in, come in," he urged while Maree gurgled her own brand of encouragement. "We can get your things after you've made yourself at home."

This would be home for a while, she thought with a surge of pleasure. Lana or no Lana, she was going to enjoy the change. If it was half as good for her as it seemed to be for Nicholas she would return to Melbourne a new woman.

She followed Nicholas along the hallway to the kitchen, which seemed to be the heart of the homestead. She realized she hadn't seen half the attractions of the lovely old home, until it came to her that last time she had made her entrance via Nicholas's bedroom. That was one room she could be sure she had seen for the last time.

"The old place is pretty impressive when you come in the front way, isn't it?" Nicholas asked over his shoulder, as if he had read her thoughts.

She was glad he didn't look back in time to catch the sudden reddening of her skin. The image of the black satin sheets was all too fresh in her mind, along with the foolish fantasy of herself in skimpy nightwear, sharing that room with him. "It's beautiful," she managed, coughing to clear the huskiness from her voice. "Has your family always lived here?"

"My great-great-grandfather built the house in the 1860s," Nicholas supplied. "He was a policeman in the goldfields but did a bit of mining in his free time. He was working his claim when a government official fell down a flooded shaft. He managed to hold the man's head above water until help came and was granted this land as a reward. My family has lived here for four generations."

She caught the sadness in his voice. "But you hadn't planned to live here?"

At the kitchen door he paused, then turned and rested his back against the wall. "Rowan—Maree's father—was my older brother, so the place rightfully belonged to him. He said it was too big to be a one-family home anymore. He planned to run it as a place where tourists could stay a few days in a tranquil, homelike atmosphere. My late sister-in-law, Kerry, was a trained chef. They would have made wonderful hosts."

His face was hidden by Maree's dark curls but his voice cracked. Bethany felt something give inside her in response and longed to tell him it was all right. He could share his pain with her if it would help. Her own recent experiences made her only too well aware of how much it hurt when a dream died.

Before she could summon the right words of comfort, the kitchen door opened and a young woman appeared framed in the opening. A little younger than Bethany, she was stunningly pretty although not as beautiful as Bethany would have expected for a model. A heart-shaped face was framed by a cascade of unruly blond curls held back from her face by a tortoiseshell comb. She was only an inch taller than Bethany herself, and her smile was warmly welcoming. "Hi, you must be Bethany, I've heard what a miracle worker you are with babies."

As soon as the door opened Nicholas straightened and smiled, although the shadows lingered around his eyes. The sight left an echo of pain around Bethany's heart, but she took her cue from him and smiled back at the young woman, enjoying the welcome that was far warmer than she'd expected for some reason. She held out her hand. "And you must be Lana Sinden. I'm glad to meet you."

Both Nicholas and the young woman frowned in unison, but the young woman spoke first. "Lana? Don't I wish.

Sorry, I'm only Kylie Ross, general dogsbody around here.''

"I told you I'd get someone in to handle the cooking and cleaning," Nicholas supplied. "Kylie's dad is the local vet. They only live five minutes away."

"So I can come over whenever I'm needed." She looked away. "My fiancé and I planned to work for Rowan and Kerry, helping to look after their guests, but now…''

"Now you work for me," Nicholas said on a deliberately upbeat note. He grinned at Bethany. "Didn't you notice a difference in my standard of housekeeping when you walked in?''

She was still recovering from the discovery that the young woman wasn't Lana Sinden. Nicholas's girlfriend hadn't returned after all. Bethany felt her spirits leap and hastily checked them. Nicholas had given no sign that he regarded her as anything other than a caretaker for Maree, so there was no point in Bethany letting her imagination run away with her. Around him she was doing far too much of that already.

"Was there something wrong with your housekeeping before?'' she asked in a carefully innocent tone.

He threw a sharp look at Kylie. "This from the woman who said her life isn't long enough to clean up after me.''

Kylie grinned. "I can't imagine why she would think that, can you?''

"Enough of this. We Frakeses know when we're outnumbered, don't we?'' he asked Maree. She gurgled a reply, and he nodded sagely. "Good idea, little darling. We'll let Kylie make Bethany a cup of coffee while I get you changed and bedded down for a nap, then I'll get Bethany settled in.''

He looked at them over the baby's dark head. "She always has good ideas.''

Was bringing Bethany here one of them? she couldn't

help wondering as she followed Kylie into the kitchen. They heard Nicholas chatting softly to the baby as he carried her off down the hall.

At her first sight of the kitchen Bethany gave a gasp. "I can't believe this is the same room." It was immaculate, the stove and cooking utensils gleaming. The floor was newly washed and polished and there wasn't a trace of spinach on Maree's spotless high chair.

"It's a slight improvement," Kylie observed, looking pleased as she uncovered a tray set with coffee things and fresh blueberry muffins on a plate. "But Nicholas is a busy man. I admire the way he transferred his business to Yarrawong and kept it going while taking care of that precious mite all on his own." She handed Bethany a cup of coffee, adding sugar in response to Bethany's prompting. "I'm glad you're here. He was starting to despair of finding someone Maree would take to."

"You didn't think of taking the job?"

Kylie grinned. "Like my father, I'm great around baby animals but hopeless around human ones."

Bethany sipped the coffee, which was delicious. "I've had a lot of practice with babies, and she's such a sweet little thing."

"That's the difference. You care about her. To the other people Nicholas interviewed, this was just a job, and not a particularly convenient one, out in the country." She gave Bethany a searching look. "Have we met before? Your name sounded familiar the moment I heard it." Then she snapped her fingers. "I know, you're the Bethany Dale who publishes *The Baby House*. My grandmother runs a craft shop in Trentham and I gave her a subscription last year for her birthday."

Bethany searched her memory. "Small Pleasures." She recalled the shop's name from a series of advertisements placed by the owner. "Your grandmother sells miniatures by mail order as well, doesn't she?"

"That's right. She makes tiny curtains, bedspreads and rugs and sometimes lampshades and other stuff for doll-house collectors. My grandmother will be thrilled when I tell her you're working here. Are you giving up publishing then?"

Bethany toyed with her coffee. "Not for good. Only until I can make the journal pay its way."

"Is that why you took this job?"

"It was part of the reason." She didn't think Nicholas would appreciate her discussing the Frakes Baby House with Kylie until they'd worked out the ground rules of her interview.

But the other woman was ahead of her. "Meeting you has reminded me. Didn't the Frakes family once have a famous dollhouse?"

Bethany shifted uncomfortably. "My favorite uncle made and collected dollhouses and told me about seeing it here, but it's no longer on public display."

"Maybe Nicholas will make an exception if you ask him about it," Kylie suggested helpfully.

"Ask Nicholas about what?" Nicholas said as he came into the kitchen. He helped himself to a muffin and regarded them with interest as he ate.

Bethany's heart sank. Now he would think she was the one who had brought up the question of the dollhouse when it was far from being his favorite subject. "Nothing that won't keep," she said dismissively, getting to her feet. "I should get my things from the car."

"We were talking about Bethany's journal and wondering about the dollhouse your family used to own," Kylie volunteered.

Bethany felt the temperature in the kitchen drop by several degrees. "Were you now? Surely you can come up with a more interesting topic of conversation than my family history?'' He dusted the crumbs off his hands and stalked out of the room.

Kylie looked worried. ''Did I say something?''

Bethany shook her head. ''No, but it's time I did.'' It was probably just as well she hadn't begun to unpack, she thought as she followed the direction Nicholas had taken. By the time she finished giving him a piece of her mind he would probably decide against hiring her, and she would be on her way back to Melbourne before she knew what hit her.

It was a risk she had to take. If the price of working here was treading on eggshells whenever Nicholas was around, she wasn't going to last long, anyway.

He was in the last place she expected to find him, lifting a bundle of clothes out of her car. She skidded to a stop, some of the wind temporarily taken out of her sails. ''What do you think you're doing?''

''Unloading your car. What does it look like?''

''Even though I'm a gossip who doesn't know when to keep her mouth shut?''

He shot her a thunderous look. ''I didn't say that.''

''You implied it when you walked out in a huff because Kylie dared to mention the dollhouse.''

Anger vibrated in his expression and stance, and he thrust the bundles back into the car before taking a step toward her, stopping only inches away. Typical male, she thought, trying to intimidate her by intruding on her personal space. If she'd been a man he would never have tried it. If she'd been a man her heart wouldn't be racing a mile a minute and her palms wouldn't be so damp she had to rub them against the sides of her slacks to dry them.

Lord but he was big. Big shoulders, big hands, big...enough of that, she reined in her errant thoughts. He was a powerfully impressive figure, especially standing so close she could feel the brush of his trouser legs against her calves. But they had a few matters to settle before she could let herself get distracted.

"I never go off in a huff," he said in a quiet voice that didn't disguise the hint of menace.

She tilted her head back to meet his eyes, which were the color of a storm-tossed sea and looked similarly dangerous. "You did a good imitation of it a few minutes ago."

"With good reason."

"Care to share it with me?"

He caught her upper arms in an implacable hold which brought them even closer together. "You already know how I feel about that damned dollhouse. You and Kylie could have talked about the weather like anybody else. Or the drive from Melbourne. Or any other neutral subject. But in the first five minutes of meeting, you have to bring up the one subject I'd rather not have discussed all over the district."

She could have pointed out that Kylie had been the one to bring up the subject, but she didn't want to get the other woman into trouble either. "You didn't exactly swear me to secrecy," she snapped, unnerved by his closeness. "In fact, you promised me an interview and photographs. Or don't you intend to honor our agreement?"

"I have every intention of honoring it," he forced out through clenched teeth. "But in my own way and time. In the meantime I'd rather you didn't splash the information all over the district."

His intensity shocked her, the effect reinforced by his grip on her arms, which would threaten her circulation if he didn't let go soon. "Why, Nicholas? What is it about the dollhouse that makes you so angry you refuse to discuss it rationally?"

His sighing breath whistled between them, but he did

slacken his hold. "Maybe I just don't want sightseers turning up on my doorstep. I had enough of it when I was growing up."

"You let me come."

"You're different. Maree likes you."

She half turned in the circle of his arms, his words provoking a surprising sense of disappointment. "Maree seems to be the only member of the family who wants me here."

"I want you here, too."

The matter-of-fact statement caught her completely off guard. "You—you do? But why? One minute you're coming down on me like a ton of bricks because of some skeleton in your family closet that you refuse to explain, and the next you say something so outrageous I don't know what to think."

"Then maybe this will help to clarify things."

His hold on her tightened again and he pulled her against him. His arms went around her shoulders, one hand threading through her hair as his lips found hers, working her mouth open gently but irresistibly. There was no time to think, react or decide whether this was a good idea before a white-hot river of desire flooded through her.

The intensity of it was so overwhelming that her knees weakened and she clung to him, feeling the world start to spin around her. Since high school she had been teased about kissing with her eyes open but this time surprise made her long lashes sweep down. Instantly she found herself in a dark cavern of pure sensation, registering every fluttering nerve and throbbing pulse on an internal Richter scale she hadn't known she possessed.

Dear heaven, if this was why most people kissed with their eyes shut she had better open hers in a hurry, she thought a little wildly, but almost closed them again as her gaze linked with his from startlingly close range.

"You keep your eyes open, too," she murmured as realization dawned.

"I like to look as well as touch," he said teasingly, his lips warm and full as they moved against her own. "This way all my five senses enjoy the experience."

Hers were almost at the point of overload, she thought. Whether it was the unexpectedness of the kiss or her own instantaneous response she didn't know. She only knew she felt light-headed from anoxia by the time he released her. At least he looked equally thunderstruck, she had the satisfaction of noticing.

He recovered first. "Now do you believe I want you to stay?"

The taste of his kiss lingered on her lips, making thinking difficult. "Are you always this persuasive, Nicholas?"

He indulged himself in a slow inspection of her from close range. His arm around her strained the soft fabric of her T-shirt, outlining the fullness of her breasts, which felt tingly from being crushed against him. "You have no idea how persuasive I can be," he murmured.

Did she really want to find out? She dropped her head but jerked it up again when her forehead brushed his chest, finding she could hardly summon her voice. "This wasn't part of our agreement."

"Wasn't it? Are you saying I was the only one who felt anything when we met?"

If she did it would be a lie, and she had a feeing he already knew it. "No," she said simply. Some part of her had known all along that whatever reasons had brought her back to Yarrawong, the most compelling of them was Nicholas himself.

"I take it you don't find me physically objectionable?" The dry mockery in his voice reminded her that she had effectively answered that question without meaning to.

She tried anyway. "You know perfectly well I don't."

In truth her own response was what alarmed her the most. No man had ever aroused her as completely as Nicholas had done in the space of a few minutes.

He put his own interpretation on the shock in her voice. "If it's what you're thinking, this isn't my usual way of auditioning caretakers for Maree."

"It never occurred to me." Surprisingly, although it probably should have.

He began to tick off points on his fingers. "Then you liked the experience, it wasn't unwelcome, and you don't think I make a habit of kissing any woman in my employ. So the only objection remaining is that it happened too fast, right?"

She managed a shaky nod, too stunned for speech. Nicholas's directness was going to take some getting used to. Among other things.

His lopsided grin warmed her like the sun on a summer day. "At least it's an objection I can remedy." His tone said he found the idea challenging, and a shiver rippled through her as she considered how he might meet the challenge.

"We'll start by getting you settled in," he continued. "No more kissing until you're ready, I promise."

It came to her that his assurance could be taken in different ways. He could mean he would wait until she indicated her readiness to be kissed again or that he could help her *get* ready. Her heartbeat went wild as the second possibility triggered a wave of heat, starting at her feet and spiraling all the way to the center of her chest.

This would have to stop, she told herself fiercely. Her response to Nicholas was purely physical. She barely knew him. She had come to Yarrawong to sort out her personal and financial problems. She didn't need any more demands on her emotions right now.

She would have to tell him so before things got any more

complicated than they were already. But not right now. After she was settled in would be soon enough. Or maybe tomorrow.

Or maybe never, she acknowledged with a silent sigh as she followed Nicholas's lead and started unpacking her car.

It wasn't until much later when she had finally finished unpacking that Bethany realized how effectively Nicholas had steered her away from the subject of the dollhouse.

Chapter Four

"**M**aybe you'll get to see a bit more of your daddy today," Bethany told Maree. Changed and fed, the baby squirmed impatiently as she was being dressed in a tiny pink T-shirt and shorts appliquéd with puffy-textured koalas. As she breathed in the sweet scents of baby powder and formula which clung to the small body, Bethany felt a tightness like a fist clenching deep inside her.

She buried her face in Maree's tummy, making soft purring noises, and the baby laughed delightedly. Bethany's vision was blurred when she lifted her head. She had always enjoyed looking after babies, but had assumed one day she would be caring for her own. It was so hard coming to terms with the idea that it wasn't going to happen.

"There will always be cuties like you who need mothering," she said to Maree in a soft voice that vibrated with the depths of her longing. Not every man rejected the idea of fathering any offspring but his own. There were men like Nicholas, for example, taking in his brother's child without a second thought and loving her as much as if he had fathered her himself.

She smiled as she pictured Nicholas with Maree. It was easy to see they shared common genes. They were both darkly attractive, stubborn as they came, and both were equally capable of spreading sunshine with the sheer force of their personalities.

She straightened. "There you are, all ready to face the day, Maree. Unfortunately that makes one of us." She tried to tell herself it wasn't because Nicholas had made himself scarce over the past few days. He had warned her of the necessity soon after she had settled into the guest wing. It seemed he had a project to complete for the Australian government, and the deadline was looming.

"Without you to help with the baby I don't know how I'd have managed," he had told her gratefully. Then he had disappeared into his office, emerging only for meals and to spend a little time with Maree before she went to sleep. Even then he was distracted, his mind obviously on his work.

Bethany knew what the problem was. The memory of his kiss still burned inside her. She wanted him to appreciate her not only for her babysitting skills but also for herself as well. It was probably foolish, considering she had been hired to care for Maree in the first place, but the feeling refused to go away.

So she was pleasantly surprised when he appeared at the door of the baby's room instead of going straight to his office, which was located in a separate building opposite the main house. "Good morning. How are my two favorite ladies this morning?"

It was a harmless enough greeting, but involuntary pleasure spilled through Bethany. She wished it was given to adults to be as spontaneous as Maree, whose baby face lit up at the sight of Nicholas. "Da, da, da, da," she chortled, stretching out her arms to him.

Nicholas reached for her and bounced her up and down in his arms. "Do you think she's trying to say Daddy?"

"First words at one year of age, sentences at two," Bethany quoted, trying to still the fast beating of her heart at the sight of him holding the infant so naturally. It was only too easy to recall the feel of those strong arms around herself. She kept her voice low, afraid its huskiness would be all too revealing. "You never know your luck."

He tickled the baby under the chin, making her laugh. "Can you say Bethany, little darling? Say it for Daddy—Beth-an-y."

"Ah, ah, ah."

"Oh well, it's a start." He hugged the child. "What would you ladies like to do today?"

Bethany shot him a startled look. Had she somehow telegraphed to him her chagrin at being left alone so much? If so, it was unintentional and she felt her face flush with remorse. "I'm supposed to leave you free to work. You don't have to take time off to entertain me."

"You know what they say about all work and no play?"

No one could accuse Nicholas of being dull, came the instantaneous thought. "But your project..."

He spread the long fingers of his free hand wide. "All finished. My final recommendations went to the government late yesterday. Now it's up to them whether they implement them or not. Until they make up their minds, I'm a free man. So I repeat, what would you like to do today?"

Bethany's thoughts spun. Spending the day in Nicholas's company was undeniably appealing, but she wasn't sure it was sensible. She had been disturbed by how much she had actually missed his presence during the past few days. Yet he had shown no sign of missing her, closeting himself with his computers and fax machines for hours on end without so much as a personal word when he finally emerged.

He had barely remembered to eat, she reminded herself.

Maybe it was normal for him to immerse himself so totally in a project. She caught her lower lip between her teeth. She knew so little about him beyond his ability to set her pulses racing with a look or a touch. Surely she had learned something from her experience with Alexander? A relationship had to be based on more than physical attraction. Their hearts had to respond to each other, as well.

Oh, for goodness' sake, he was only suggesting a day's outing, probably more for Maree's sake than mine, she told herself impatiently. Why was she making such a big deal out of it? "We could go to Trentham and visit Kylie's grandmother's craft shop," she said firmly, voicing the first suggestion springing to mind.

"Good idea. It's a short drive but there are some pleasant walks through the State Forest out that way...so put on your walking shoes." He jiggled Maree in his arms. "What do you think, little darling? Would you like to go bush walking?"

"You'd better take a long leash," Bethany advised. "She's started discovering her sea legs and wants to use them at every opportunity."

His face fell. "Don't tell me I missed her first steps?"

"Nothing so ambitious. At the moment she's more into wriggling, rolling, crawling and creeping, accompanied by a lot of toppling over. But it won't be long before she discovers proper walking."

"No wonder she's so squirmy all of a sudden. You can't wait to get down and explore, can you? Just don't start walking while we're in the bush, will you?"

In spite of the tension winding through her, Bethany was forced to laugh. "Relax. She won't suddenly jump up and go jogging. She has lots more experimenting to do before she gets the hang of this walking business."

Like me, Bethany couldn't help thinking. Where Nicholas was concerned she could do well to take a lesson from the baby, letting herself crawl before she tried to walk. Baby steps, she remembered one of the psychologists at the shelter advising, when Bethany consulted her about a work-related problem. Take things one step at a time like baby steps. She had applied the advice to herself after finding out she couldn't have children, schooling herself to think only as far as the next day and the next until the initial shock became more bearable. It was good advice for handling this situation, too.

With Nicholas it was easier said than done, she discovered, as they set off in his four-wheel-drive vehicle along the Old Calder Highway. Maree was safely strapped into a baby seat in the back, and Bethany was relieved that the baby showed no fear of traveling in a car, despite her previous tragic experience.

At the Kyneton mineral springs Nicholas turned off toward the Coliban River, a former gold boom area, he informed her. She absorbed the information with a sense of detachment, much more aware of Nicholas himself than the history he was imparting. When he stretched out a hand to point out the ruins of the original river crossing, lying on the bed of the stream next to the bridge they were on, she nodded dutifully. But she was more conscious of the way the corded muscles of his arm, which was bare below his rolled-back shirtsleeve, brushed her forearm in passing. In fascination she noticed the pattern of blue veins near the surface of his skin and had to resist the urge to trace them with her finger.

Baby steps, she reminded herself fiercely, making an effort to rein in her runaway imagination. She wasn't usually so fanciful where men were concerned. It must be the aftereffects of ending her recent relationship that was making her so aware of Nicholas as a man, she decided. Somehow the answer was less than wholly satisfying.

Nicholas parked the car near the bridge and looked over

his shoulder at Maree. "Here's where we find out what those gorgeous legs can do."

"I hope you don't mean it literally," Bethany said in alarm. "She isn't steady enough on her feet yet to do any actual walking."

Humor sparkled in the glance he shared with her. "I wasn't referring to Maree."

"Oh, I see. I assumed..."

He grinned. "That because I've been tied up with work, I haven't noticed what your legs do for a pair of shorts?"

She *had* assumed he was too preoccupied to notice what she wore, and the discovery that he had, brought the color surging to her face. "It's been too hot to wear anything else."

"It also provided the perfect incentive to get the government project finished as soon as possible so I could get out of my office and into a pair of shorts with you."

As soon as he realized what he'd said he burst out laughing. "Darn it, you know what I mean. We'd better hit the road before I get myself into more trouble."

She knew very well that his comment was no more than a slip of the tongue, but it didn't dispel her sense of wonder that she had been on his mind while he was working so intensely. So it wasn't all on her side. Although she tried to curb her soaring spirits, the thought lent her feet wings as she helped to unload the car.

Nicholas had asked Kylie to prepare some picnic food for their lunch. It was packed into a backpack with a built-in baby seat which Nicholas could carry easily on his shoulders. Bethany helped to strap Maree into the safety harness then popped a cotton sun hat onto her dark head and a wide-brimmed straw one onto her own. Bethany carried a lightweight backpack that held everything the baby might need.

They could be any normal happy family setting off on

an outing, she thought as she followed Nicholas along a quiet graveled road on the western bank of the river. The sun filtering down on them through the thick eucalyptus forest added to her holiday mood. For the first time in a long while her heart felt light.

The track skirted a reservoir, and Maree bounced up and down in delight as she caught sight of a group of waterbirds wading in the shallows. A cart track led them down into a shallow gully then along a fence line to a ridge crest where Bethany drew a deep breath of pure pleasure as she saw the profusion of wildflowers in bloom. "It's simply beautiful," she commented.

Nicholas seemed pleased by her enthusiasm. "I thought you'd appreciate it. Rowan and I used to walk here every chance we got when we were growing up."

"You must miss him a lot," she observed, looking sadly at Maree's small head resting against Nicholas's in the baby carrier. She tried to imagine how she would feel if anything happened to Sam or Joanie, or any of her foster siblings. She hoped she would be as strong as Nicholas, who was obviously saddened to the depths of his being, but carried on out of respect for his brother and sister-in-law's memories as well as for the sake of the baby bequeathed to his care.

"That's why I like the forest," he commented in a low voice. "Rowan and Kerry are never more alive to me than here, where we shared so many good times. I want Maree to grow up in the same places her parents did, as a way of keeping in touch with their memory in a happy way."

Bethany regarded him through glistening eyes. "It's a beautiful idea. Most men would never think of such a thing."

The look he gave her burned with intensity. "Haven't you realized it yet? I'm not most men."

She'd known it from the moment they met, and she low-

ered her lashes to avoid letting her eyes betray her certainty.
"I think we'd better stop for lunch." In the bush with only
the baby for a chaperone, it would be far too easy to admit
that he affected her more than any man she'd ever encoun-
tered, and she was far from ready for where such an admission might lead.

They were skirting the western end of the Lauriston Reservoir. Exotic trees grew in landscaped surroundings at the
end of the dam wall, which Nicholas told her dated from
1938. Across the dam was a picnic area located on a small
promontory with views of the water. It was the perfect
place to unpack the chicken rolls, fresh strawberries and
cold drinks Kylie had provided for their lunch.

For Maree there was a flask of pureed chicken and veg-
etables and another of peach slivers in whipped yogurt.
After her morning in the fresh air the baby made short work
of her lunch, then allowed Bethany to change her before
she settled down for a nap on a rug in the shade of a tree.

Bethany leaned against the trunk of the same tree and
watched the baby sleep. "Why do small creatures tug at
our heartstrings so?" she pondered aloud.

He dropped to the rug beside her. "Because they're helpless and innocent, and they need us," he observed.

She regarded him through half-closed eyes. "My boss at
the children's shelter says we're genetically programmed to
care about small creatures to ensure the survival of the spe-
cies."

"But you don't believe it?" He answered the doubt he
heard in her voice.

She shook her head. "If it were true, then everyone
would feel the same. But the parents of the kids needing
shelter contradict the theory. We had one little boy..." She
let her voice trail off, suddenly afraid of revealing too much
of herself to him.

He would have none of her hesitation. "You can't stop now. Go on."

"He was too old for the shelter and too young for the available crisis accommodation. His parents didn't want him at home so I took him home with me for a week, until we could find a foster home for him."

She was aware of Nicholas's gaze softening. "I'll bet you take in stray kittens as well."

She lowered her lashes over misty eyes. "How'd you guess?"

He touched a finger to her face and caught a bead of moisture under one eye. "This, for starters. I hate the thought of your work causing you this much pain."

His arms came around her and his mouth found hers with unerring precision. What began as a kiss of comfort, rapidly turned into something deeper, making her thoughts spin with the wonder of it. Kissing him back with equal passion felt like the most natural thing in the world. When he pulled away, her heart was pounding like a kangaroo in full flight.

His voice was husky as he said, "We'd better get moving if we're to call on Kylie's grandmother at her shop."

The return to reality came as a shock. He wouldn't have kissed her at all if she hadn't started talking about the kids at the shelter, she told herself, making an inward resolution to guard her emotions more carefully next time. Wearing her heart on her sleeve was distinctly risky with Nicholas around.

He set a brisk pace back to the car where Bethany was glad to collapse into the front seat and catch her breath while Nicholas secured Maree in her safety seat in the back. The country air had also taken a toll on the baby, who was sound asleep again.

As Nicholas had promised, Trentham was only a short drive away, and they were soon driving down High Street with its collection of quaint buildings shaded by wooden verandahs, cafés and stores offering country-style food-stuffs and a variety of handicrafts and original textile products by local artists.

"No wonder Kylie's grandmother opened her shop here," Bethany observed as they passed a center offering cast-iron lacework and ornaments from the Victorian era. Another turnoff brought them to a store whose hand-painted sign identified it as Small Pleasures.

"It's so tiny," Bethany exclaimed, admiring the store, which could be no more than a dozen feet wide with two windows, like eyes, crammed with miniature merchandise.

"Probably why she chose the name," Nicholas agreed. "You go inside. I'll stay here with Maree. She's sleeping so soundly it's a shame to wake her up."

"Don't you want to meet Kathryn Ross?"

"We've met at local social activities. She'll understand that teeny tiny merchandise is not really my thing."

Did it have something to do with his aversion to the Frakes Baby House? she couldn't help wondering. "I'll try not to take too long," she promised.

He slid back in the driver's seat and tilted his Akubra hat over his eyes. "Take as long as you like. Maree and I will be fine."

All the same she felt a twinge of unease as she walked into the little shop. A bell tinkled to announce her arrival, and a woman emerged from the back, wiping her hands on a checkered apron as she came. Her smile broadened when she caught sight of her customer. "Don't tell me, you're Bethany Dale who's working for Nicholas Frakes."

"Yes, but how did you—"

"My Kylie gave me a pretty accurate description of you, including how lovely you are," Mrs. Ross explained. "But even if she hadn't I'd have recognized you from the picture in your journal."

It was only a postage-stamp-sized likeness, but Bethany

felt flattered by Mrs. Ross's comments and Kylie's favorable report. "It's wonderful to meet you. I've wanted to do an article on your work since I first heard about it from other collectors."

Mrs. Ross nodded, looking pleased. "I got a lot of orders for my dollhouse accessories after those advertisements you ran, so an article would give my business a big boost."

"Then I'll set it up while I'm here," Bethany promised.

Mrs. Ross frowned. "You aren't planning to stay at Yarrawong?"

Bethany shook her head. "I'm only caring for Maree until Nicholas finds someone permanent."

"What a shame. From what my Kylie said I thought you and Nicholas...well, you know."

Bethany felt the heat travel from her neck into her face. Gossip usually spread like wildfire in the country, but she had never dreamed people were already pairing her off with Nicholas. "It isn't like that at all," she said firmly. "I need the job to help me keep the journal afloat and Nicholas offered me the work so—here I am." The explanation sounded forced even to her own ears, but it was the truth, whether other people chose to believe it or not. That it might not be the whole explanation, Bethany didn't care to consider.

Mrs. Ross nodded. "If you say so, dear. But Nicholas is a fine man and you could do a lot worse. If my granddaughter wasn't engaged..."

No doubt half the parents and grandparents in the Central Highlands had entertained the same thought. Why hadn't Nicholas dated any of the local girls, Bethany wondered briefly, then dismissed the thought. Until a few months ago he had lived in Melbourne, and his love life had been occupied with the lovely Lana Sinden. Since returning to Yarrawong he'd had his hands full with his work and looking after Maree. But he wouldn't allow himself to be lonely for long, and when he did decide to get back into circulation, Bethany had a feeling every single woman in the district would be beating a path to his door.

She banished the thought by prowling around the tiny shop and inspecting the hundreds of miniatures on display, eventually selecting several pieces for her own dollhouse at home. She was particularly taken with Mrs. Ross's hand-made rugs, quilts and curtain sets which were finer than anything she'd seen at collectors' fairs.

"You must come to my workroom out the back and see the photos my customers have sent me," the elderly woman urged.

Bethany glanced through the front window to where Nicholas waited in the car. He was still slumped in the front seat with his hat over his eyes. Surely he wouldn't mind her taking another few minutes? "I'd love to," she agreed.

The workroom was even smaller and more crowded than the shop, but she waved away Mrs. Ross's apology for the chaos. "It's worth a little clutter to produce the miniature marvels you do," she said. "It's hard to believe you make everything yourself in this tiny workshop."

"Every one," Mrs. Ross confirmed proudly. "Ever since Mr. Ross passed away I've devoted every waking hour to my little world. It's worth it when I get letters from all over Australia and photos like these, showing where my work ends up."

She gestured toward a wall of photographs of every kind of dollhouse imaginable, some with the owners posed proudly in front, others open to display the contents. Suddenly she put a finger to her mouth. "I have some photos here you should find particularly interesting." She delved beneath layers of photos to produce three of patently older vintage, faded and curling at the corners. "Here, what do you think of these?"

Bethany studied the photos. They showed a dollhouse

from the last century, complete with intricately detailed period furniture. "It's magnificent," she agreed.

Mrs. Ross swelled with pride, making Bethany think the heirloom must belong to her family, until she said, "It's the Frakes Baby House which used to be in Nicholas's family. I saw it when I was a child, but we moved away and I haven't heard anything of it for years. Maybe you can get Nicholas to tell you more about it." She lowered her voice conspiratorially. "Although after what happened, I can understand him being sensitive about it."

She folded her arms and leaned closer as if eager to share the details with Bethany. Fighting her rising curiosity, Bethany shook her head. "If he wants me to know, I'm sure he'll tell me in his own time."

Mrs. Ross looked unperturbed. "Don't be surprised if he doesn't, dear. It wasn't exactly a happy time for young Nicholas. He…"

At the sound of a cough, she broke off. Nicholas himself was framed in the doorway of the workroom. He was carrying Maree, and he looked as angry as Bethany had ever seen him.

Mrs. Ross didn't seem to notice. "Nicholas, how nice. We were just talking about you."

It was the second time he had interrupted Bethany apparently discussing him behind his back, and his furious expression said he was unlikely to believe that Bethany was innocent of starting it on both occasions. "Mrs. Ross has some wonderful old photos of the Frakes Baby House," Bethany said brightly, attempting to salvage the situation.

"You can have them if you like, since the house belonged to your family," Mrs. Ross offered, holding out the yellowing photographs.

Hefting Maree into one arm, he took the photos as if they could bite. "Maybe Bethany would like them since the house is of such consuming interest to her," he said coldly.

She wanted to beg him not to talk about her in such a disparaging tone. She hadn't sought the photos nor encouraged Mrs. Ross to gossip. But the damage was done. He was clearly furious that the subject had arisen at all. "We'd better go, Maree will be hungry again soon," she told the other woman.

Oblivious to the undercurrents swirling around her, Mrs. Ross beamed at the baby. "Of course. Poor little mite. It's just as well she has you, Nicholas, or she'd be all alone in the world."

"That's one thing she will never be," he said in such a savage undertone that Bethany regarded him in astonishment. Other than bringing up the touchy subject of the Frakes Baby House, what on earth had Mrs. Ross said to provoke such a reaction?

"Thank you for showing me around. I'll call you to arrange an interview about your work," she emphasized in case Nicholas thought she intended to press Mrs. Ross for more details about his family. It was becoming obvious that there was a scandal attached to the Frakes Baby House but the only person she wanted to hear it from was Nicholas himself, and after today he was more likely to send her packing back to Melbourne than to share his family secrets with her.

He maintained an icy silence as he settled Maree in her car seat but when he slid behind the wheel he turned to Bethany, his expression thunderous. "You won't be happy until you know the whole sordid story, will you?"

This was too much. "Nicholas, whatever you think, I didn't ask Mrs. Ross about the Frakes house. It was her idea to show me the photos, so you have no cause to be angry with me."

He slammed his palms against the steering wheel. "I

noticed you didn't exactly discourage her from discussing it.''

"Discussing what? She hinted at some scandal attached to the house but that's all.''

He swung sideways to face her, his eyes glittering dangerously. ''Then allow me to enlighten you. I have no time for the Frakes Baby House, as you call it, because it all but destroyed my family.''

Chapter Five

Bethany laced her fingers tightly together. "Please don't do this, Nicholas."

"Don't do what? Give you what you came for? My only question is, what will you do once you've got it?"

"I don't understand."

He strained the words through his teeth. "Once I give you the story you came for, will you stay or will you up and leave?"

Not long ago the answer would have been obvious. She had come to Yarrawong to find the long-lost Frakes Baby House. Now she was on the brink of succeeding, she wasn't sure what she wanted any more. The story was important to her, crucial as a means of getting out of debt and saving her journal. But she knew it wasn't why she wanted to stay.

"I agreed to take care of Maree until you find someone permanent and I will, story or no story," she said quietly, knowing it was far from being the whole truth. Nicholas himself was the reason she couldn't imagine walking away. She had never met such a complex man—one moment playfully relaxed, the next as darkly fascinating and fearsome as a moonless landscape. The thought of exploring that unknown territory both excited and scared her but she was afraid it was already too late to go back. In allowing Nicholas to kiss her once she had already taken the first steps.

Another thought came to her, and tension knifed through her as she added, "If you still want me here, that is."

"Bethany." The word was so low and harsh it was barely recognizable as her own name. He steered the car off the road into the shadow of a pine forest, snapped off the engine and his seat belt before unfastening her seat belt in a swift series of movements.

His actions were so decisive that she had no time to think before he reached for her. Fueled by his anger, his touch was more demanding than gentle, yet she was unable to stop her heartbeat becoming a frantic flutter as soon as he gathered her roughly into his arms.

The warmth flooding her limbs owed nothing to the heat of the day and everything to how much she welcomed the feel of his arms around her. It also explained the whirlpool of confusing sensations eddying through her as he kissed her. A moment ago he had been furious with her and she had been afraid that his anger spelled the end of any chance to experience his touch again. Now his lips moved against hers with a fierceness that ignited her blood like a fever.

She didn't want to think about anything except how good it felt to be kissed by him, but her mind insisted on replaying his angry declaration about the baby house destroying his family.

Another unwelcome thought took hold in her mind. The first time Nicholas had kissed her they'd been discussing the house, too. A fearful pressure gripped her heart, demanding her attention. If this was his way of distracting her, it was more effective than it had any right to be. It also meant the embrace was a fraud.

As if he sensed her withdrawal he released her slowly. When he returned to his own side of the car she was aware of an internal emptiness that hadn't been there before he kissed her, as if she had given up something precious. She knew her face was pale as she followed him with her eyes, the last flutters of her accelerated heartbeat lending her voice a faint tremor. "Nicholas, why did you do that?"

He looked away to the shifting shadows of the surrounding bush. "Have you seen your reflection in a mirror lately?"

She refused to let the implied compliment sidetrack her. "I mean kiss me when we were arguing about the dollhouse?"

His pewter gaze flamed as he swung around to glare at her. "It wasn't to change the subject under discussion, if that's what you're saying, although as distractions go it was pretty effective."

Perhaps he'd done it without conscious intention. "This is the second time it's happened," she pointed out uneasily.

"Is it? Maybe it's because a heated discussion with you gets my blood racing, and I lose just enough control to do something I won't let myself do when I'm thinking more clearly."

The thought that she affected him to such an extent made her head spin for a moment, and she reached out for something to steady herself. The nearest support happened to be Nicholas's arm. As soon as her fingers closed on his firm, warm flesh and she felt the fine hairs on his forearm teasing her palm, she knew exactly what he meant about losing control.

He felt it, too, she noticed as his breathing became faster and shallower, mimicking hers. He turned his arm so her hand slid into his and their fingers interwove. "Would it help if I kissed you without getting mad at you first?"

She dragged in a deep breath but still felt oxygen deprived. "It might not work. Perhaps we're the kind of people who need to have a fight before they can..."

"Make love?" he supplied when her voice trailed away.

She almost choked. "I was going to say 'be honest with each other.'"

He gave a lazy grin, his fingers threading in and out of hers in a dance that sent shafts of delicious sensation spearing to the center of her being. "I like my answer better."

A muffled protest came from the back seat, followed by quiet whimpering. Nicholas gave a sigh. "Either way, we aren't going to find out right now. It sounds as if the baby's awake."

Not only awake but hungry and fractious, Bethany found when she got out to investigate. Kylie had supplied enough flasks of baby food to satisfy Maree's immediate needs, but she insisted on feeding herself so it was a slow, messy process. In a curious way Bethany welcomed the distraction. It gave her the time she needed to collect her scattered wits and get her runaway emotions under control.

Whatever Nicholas said, his actions spoke differently. He had kissed her twice, and on both occasions he was furious with her for raising the subject of the baby house. She didn't really believe they were the type of people who needed to be angry in order to be passionate. At least she wasn't. Again she lacked basic information to draw such conclusions about his character. But instinct and the experience of seeing him interact with the baby told Bethany he was more civilized than that. She was willing to bet he wouldn't be a shrinking violet in bed, but he didn't strike her as a caveman, either.

She was glad to be occupied with cleaning and changing the baby so Nicholas couldn't see her expression, which felt as if it was beet red. Even if he was a caveman it was no business of hers. Two kisses under adverse conditions hardly made her an expert on his romantic tendencies, and he had shown no signs of wanting any more from her. She was letting her fantasies run away with her again. Around Nicholas it was becoming a bad habit.

She was glad of the drive back to Yarrawong, which gave her chance to reestablish some kind of emotional control, at least outwardly. Inside was another matter.

"Where are we going?" she asked when Nicholas directed her toward the building that housed his office. Waiting to greet them at the front door, Kylie had gladly taken charge of Maree, and the two of them had already gone inside. When Bethany started to follow, Nicholas had steered her toward the outbuilding.

"I'm about to give you what you wanted," he said tautly.

"You're going to show me the baby house now?"

"Will I have any peace until I do?"

Despair washed over her. "We've been over this. It isn't my fault that Mrs. Ross brought the subject up and frankly, I don't care if I never see the house if it's such a source of pain to you." She would find some other way to solve her problem.

His startled look raked her features. "You're serious, aren't you?"

"I don't want to hurt you, Nicholas."

His pace slowed. "You won't. My reaction today tells me it's time I dragged this thing into the light, so you could be doing me a favor."

He didn't sound as if it was a favor, but he was determined to see it through. Trying to change his mind once it was made up was as futile as trying to hold back the waters of the Coliban River by main force. With a sigh she quickened her pace to keep up with his long strides.

When she first arrived he had told her he had converted an old coach house into his office. It was a two-story building with a hayloft above it, a short distance away from the main house. Outwardly it looked every bit of its hundred and thirty years, with a heavy oak door that creaked when Nicholas opened it. But first he had to disable a modern alarm system, reminding her of the classified nature of his work.

Inside were more reminders in the shape of state-of-the-art computers and other equipment she couldn't identify. There was little of the coach house atmosphere remaining here. The rough-hewn boards had been lined and painted a gleaming ivory, but the floorboards remained uncovered, polished to a glowing patina. A pair of telephones had gadgets attached to them, presumably for extra security. In curious contrast to the messy state of his housekeeping pre-Kylie, this place was a model of neatness and order.

The only place where chaos reigned was a corner fenced off by a childproof barrier behind which was a collection of brightly colored toys and cuddly animals. "For Maree?"

He nodded. "When I couldn't find a nanny, I started bringing her in with me while I worked. She enjoys the bright lights and chirping sounds of the equipment, and I talk to her. Sometimes if I'm stuck on a project I get in there with her and we play together. It blows the cobwebs away and she adores it."

The image of Nicholas playing baby games with Maree behind the barrier brought a lump to Bethany's throat. It wasn't that she couldn't imagine him down on the floor playing This Little Piggy Went to Market. She could imagine it all too vividly, and a longing for such a simple, elemental experience with her own child tore through her and she turned away to avoid letting him see her distress.

He misunderstood her sudden withdrawal. "I realize this isn't what you want to see." He directed her toward a tim-

ber staircase leading to the loft. It wasn't the original staircase, being too modern and sturdy, but upstairs was another
matter. The loft looked as if it was a repository for everything the household no longer used. Period furniture, old
trunks and framed pictures peeped out from under dustcov-
ers. It wasn't really dusty. In fact the area was spotlessly
clean in deference to the computer equipment in the lower
room. But the impression was of a rarely visited attic, and
she had to suppress an urge to sneeze at the dust, which
existed only in her imagination.

She waited at the head of the stairs as Nicholas went to
one of the covers and pulled it away. "This is what you
wanted, isn't it?"

A cry of astonishment was wrenched from her. "Nicholas, it's beautiful." The dollhouse was the most perfect
example of colonial architecture in miniature she had ever
seen. It stood about two and a half feet tall and almost four
feet wide with a colonnaded portico supporting a balcony.
The windows were evenly spaced in the style favored by
English designers of the post-Waterloo period.

The entire front opened to reveal a Palladian villa in
miniature.

She dropped to her knees and peered into the central
staircase saloon, which had an arcade circling it on the floor
above. The saloon's flagging floor was designed to look
like sandstone, while brass hardware and cedar joinery
faithfully reproduced the style of the period. Eight perfectly
proportioned rooms opened off the saloon.

A dining room had dark red walls and Victorian-style
mahogany furniture. A perfect replica of an 1841 John
Broadwood piano looked as if it could be played, and a
tiny marble fireplace surrounded a perfectly set fire, await-
ing only the touch of a match to bring it to flickering life.

"I've never seen anything like it," she said hoarsely,
touching each small piece of furniture with a fingertip. It

was a faithful record in miniature of life in early Australia during the colonial period. How could anyone hide away such a treasure? But when her entranced gaze went to Nicholas's face she was shocked to find none of the awe she felt, but only cold rejection of the house and its marvelous contents.

She closed up the house and stumbled to her feet. "What is it, Nicholas? You said this house almost destroyed your family."

He threw aside another dustcover, revealing a carved love seat which his gesture invited her to use. Instead of joining her he began to pace the length of the loft. "There's not a lot to tell, and perhaps it's less dramatic than my memories want to make it. The dollhouse was made for my great-great-grandmother by one of the colonial architects who also designed Elizabeth Bay House. When I was a boy the thing was kept in a place of honor in the formal living room."

Now Bethany understood why the design looked so familiar. Elizabeth Bay House still stood on the shores of Sydney Harbour, and historical records described it as "the finest house in the colony." If the Frakes Baby House was modeled on it, it was a find indeed.

But to her surprise she found the house concerned her less than Nicholas's reaction to it. "What happened?" she prompted, releasing the breath she was unaware she'd been holding. She felt as if she stood outside a locked door and Nicholas held the key. Opening it would either bring them closer together or drive them apart for all time, she sensed.

He pulled in a deep breath. "Word got around about it, and people frequently came asking to see it. My mother loved the company and was happy to show it off to anyone who came by, but Dad hated strangers dropping in. After my grandparents died he wanted to pack the house away out of public view. It was the source of more arguments between my parents than anything else.''

It was an unpleasant association but it hardly explained the extent of his aversion to the lovely object, she thought. She schooled herself to silence, sure Nicholas had more to tell her.

She was right. ''When I was about eleven, a man called from Sydney to ask if he could see the dollhouse. My father was away but my mother encouraged the visit.'' There was a long pause before Nicholas said in a low voice, ''He came several times, supposedly to see the house. I didn't realize it was my mother he really wanted to see until the day she ran away with him. She never came back.''

''You can't think there was anything you could have done?'' Bethany offered, although it was obvious that Nicholas did think so. There was self-reproach in every line of his expression.

He dragged stiff fingers through his short-cropped hair. ''It hardly matters now, does it? She and the man moved to England, and the only contact we have is an occasional card at Christmas.''

''How did your father take it?''

Nicholas's answering look was bleak. ''He was never exactly outgoing, but after she left he withdrew completely into a shell and wouldn't let anyone near him emotionally. It took him another ten years to complete the job, but I believe he began to die from the time my mother told him she was leaving.''

Coming from a large, supportive family herself, she found it hard to imagine how lonely life must have been for Nicholas and his brother, abandoned by their mother and cut off from their father by the depth of his own grief. No wonder he found no joy in the dollhouse which had brought only misery to his family. ''Didn't your father have friends or relatives he could turn to?''

Nicholas shook his head, his eyes like chips of ice. "There's only his sister who lives in Queensland and has a large family. Rowan and I spent occasional holidays with her, but Dad preferred to stay here alone. Thank goodness Aunt Edna showed us that it wasn't normal to cocoon yourself away from the rest of society, otherwise Rowan and I might have turned into hermits like our father."

She hadn't known Rowan, but his plans to turn Yarrawong into a bed and breakfast for travelers suggested he had been far from hermitlike. And Nicholas wasn't the type to cut himself off from life, she would swear to it. She had never met a man with a greater zest for living or a more powerful ability to love. Her own brief taste of his passion filled her with a yearning so strong it took her breath away. "I don't think you have it in you," she denied softly.

His eyebrow angled upward cynically. "So you're an expert on my character now?"

She linked her hands in her lap to conceal her rising tension. "Two kisses hardly make me an expert."

Some of the coldness left his expression, and he took a step toward her, his pewter eyes glittering a challenge. "That sounds a lot like an invitation, Bethany."

She hadn't intended it as one, at least not consciously, but in any case it was too late. He loomed over her on the love seat, planting an arm on either side of her body, effectively trapping her. When she started to rise, his arms closed around her and he lifted her against him. She felt his strength melt whatever resistance she might have offered.

"What are you doing?" she whispered around a throat tight with emotion.

"Making you an expert on Nicholas Devlin Frakes," he ground out, tasting her with his lips between each word until she trembled with the delicious eroticism of it.

She wasn't alone, she realized as she felt his body harden

against her. Desire more powerful than anything she'd ever experienced roared through her, starting somewhere at the base of her spine and surging all the way to the top of her head. Her gasp of astonishment opened her mouth against his, and he made the most of the chance to weave a dance of delight around the moist cavern with his tongue.

She didn't pull back although distantly there was the thought that she should. It was far more pleasurable to answer his kisses with her own, while his hands played a melody of tactile delight along her spine.

Nicholas felt his own senses start to spin. He had meant to demonstrate that Bethany was no expert on his innermost feelings. Women always thought they understood a man as soon as they learned a few things about his history. He had read it in her face as he told her about his mother running off with the man who came to see the dollhouse. Bethany had decided instantly that it was the reason why he hated the house.

It would never occur to her that he hated the role it had played in destroying his father, more than anything it had done to Nicholas himself. Long before his mother ran away she had used the house as leverage to annoy his father. The more his dad had objected to strangers traipsing through their home, the more his mother had put out the welcome mat. The baby house, as Bethany called it, was a symbol of everything that had been amiss in his parents' marriage, and that was why he didn't want it in his sight.

He had kissed her by way of making a point, never expecting his heartbeat to start pounding as if he'd run a marathon or to have a hunger so strong it was like a drug ripping through his system. It threw him completely off center.

Logic demanded he release her and apologize for letting things get out of hand. But they were already so far out of hand that letting her go was the last thing on his mind. He bent his head and kissed the sweet hollow of her throat just above the inviting shadow between her breasts. Her T-shirt had escaped the waistband of her jeans, and a whimper of pleasure leaped from her throat as he slid his hand upward to gently explore her feminine fullness.

Her skin reminded him of ice cream, smooth-textured and creamy, and rich as sin. Raiding the freezer for a spoonful of the frozen treat when no one was looking had been one of his guilty pleasures as a child. There was the same sense of dipping into something forbidden now as his questing fingers located one tiny peak of hardness and rubbed it between thumb and forefinger, then bestowed the same attention to its twin. She gasped, and he felt her shudder resonate through his own body.

He no longer wanted to teach her anything except how good it would feel when they made love, he thought dizzily. He felt as if he was about to explode with the force of his arousal, and he didn't doubt she felt the same way. The couch was behind her, practically inviting him to press her down onto it and show her how to reach up and pull down the stars from the sky.

Except that this wasn't the place. He wanted to make love to Bethany more than he had wanted anything in a long time, but when it happened he wanted it to be special. Not rough and ready, in a loft filled with unhappy memories.

Even so it took all the resolve he possessed to set her away from him, holding on to her until he was sure her legs were steady enough. Her pupils were huge and black, and there was a red mark on her throat from his mouth. He traced it with his thumb pad, and she looked at him in a daze, her hands trembling slightly. "Why did you stop?"

"I never should have started," he growled.

She misunderstood he saw as soon as the words were out of his mouth. "So you think it's all a mistake?"

"I didn't say any such thing. I brought you up here to look at a dollhouse, not to seduce you, not now, anyway."

Her head came up, her eyes widening until she reminded him of one of the wild bush creatures. "I'm not sure it's a good idea now—or any other time," she said with unsteady emphasis. "You admitted the dollhouse has nothing but bad associations for you. Yet collecting them and writing about them is my work and my avocation."

"Then maybe it's time I changed my opinion of them," he said in a low voice, surprising both of them, himself most of all. "You could be just what I need to make the change work."

She looked shakily pleased but lifted her hand and gnawed the back of one knuckle. "I'm not sure I care to be used as therapy."

The gesture did such extraordinary things to his insides that he almost wrapped his arms around her again. He held himself back by sheer effort of will. "You won't be used at all, Bethany. Not by me or any other man. Whatever we decide to do will be by mutual consent, and I promise you it will be unforgettable."

He was afraid he'd alarmed her when he saw her mouth drop open, although she must have been as aware of the electricity crackling between them as he was. A moment ago they'd practically been incinerated by it. "I'd better go and get Maree. It's almost time for Kylie to go home."

"What's the matter, Bethany?" Her eyes, which had been bright with passion, were still softly luminous. She looked edgy, as if she almost—but not quite—regretted the last few minutes. Then he cursed himself for being an idiot. "Is there someone at home for you?"

Her head came up. "No, there's no one."

"But there was?" He was fishing, but instinct told him he was on the right track.

"For a while I thought there was. I was wrong."

"It ended badly?"

"My mistake was in thinking it ever really started."

She moved toward the staircase, but he forestalled her with a gesture. "You stay here and take a good look through the dollhouse. I'll look after Maree. It is my day off," he reminded her when she started to protest about it being her job. "Take all the time you like. I'll call you when dinner's ready."

She gave in without an argument, probably because she couldn't wait to examine that blasted house, he guessed. What was it with women and miniature things? Every woman who'd ever crossed the threshold of Yarrawong had gone weak over the house. Maybe it brought out their maternal instincts or something.

It sure didn't bring out his, he thought as he bounded down the stairs and crossed the cobbled courtyard to the main house. In the loft with Bethany, the house had been the last thing on his mind. It showed how powerfully she distracted him, when he had stopped noticing it was there.

He should have known there was a man in her recent past. She was too beautiful and sweet not to be fighting them off in droves. It sounded as if there was only one, past tense. Nor did it take a psychologist to work out that she had been hurt when it ended. She had said she didn't want to be therapy for Nicholas over the dollhouse, but maybe they could help each other. He had a feeling he was just the tonic she needed to get over that affair that "hadn't really started."

Telling himself it was for her, he began to plan the evening. First he would get Maree fed and settled for the night. With luck and a day of fresh air, she would sleep soundly tonight. Then he would prepare a dinner guaranteed to take Bethany's mind off any man but himself.

Candles, they needed candles, he thought as he put the finishing touches to the meal an hour or so later. He found candles in a drawer in the dining room, but there were no holders, so he dropped a couple of shot glasses into the center of a bowl of flowers Kylie had put on the table and supported the candles in them. The effect was sure to impress Bethany, he decided, standing back to admire his handiwork.

Humming under his breath he dimmed the room lights and went to fetch his dinner companion.

"It looks wonderful," she enthused when he led her into the dining room. "I have to change. This deserves more than a T-shirt and jeans."

"Make it quick, dinner's almost ready," he said. It hadn't occurred to him to give her time to dress up. He was perfectly happy with what she had on, especially the way it outlined the full, high curves of her breasts, but he kept the opinion to himself.

He was glad he had, when she emerged a scant ten minutes later wearing a short black number that did even more amazing things for her shape. The dress had a heart-shaped front and spaghetti straps which crossed over in a pattern above the low-cut back. During the day the sun had kissed her skin with gold. It was all he could do to keep his mind on serving their dinner of fine pasta with a local delicacy made of pork and beef marinated in red wine and seasoned with pepper and spices, and a salad of greens from his own garden.

The wine was a particularly good Shiraz from Craiglea winery, close to Melbourne. For dessert he had a selection of berries from the Musk Valley, served with fresh brandy cream.

He lifted his glass to her. "To a woman I knew was

special from the time she first walked through my bed-room.'' It was the literal truth, but her color heightened at the reminder. It was a long time since he'd known a female who blushed as prettily as Bethany did, and it brought out all his he-man protective instincts.

"I only walked through it because the front door was locked. I didn't stay there," she protested.

"A problem I'll happily rectify," he said, meeting her eyes over the rim of his wineglass. In the flickering light of the candles she looked tiny and ethereal, like an angel at his table. He only hoped he was right and there was a touch of devil there, too.

She forked some beef into her mouth which was outlined in shell pink tonight. "This is delicious."

"You're changing the subject."

She shook her head. "I'm appreciating your talents."

His look was slow and measured. "Believe me, the feeling is very, very mutual."

Unfortunately Maree chose that moment to stand up in her crib again, the sound of her activities amplified by the speaker system connecting her room with the living room. They both rose at the same moment. "I'll go."

He grinned at the chorus. "We'll go together."

For the third time since he'd put her to bed Maree was holding on to the sides of the bed. "I know you can stand, little darling. You're amazing, but do you have to practice in the middle of the night?" he grumbled.

Bethany moved him gently to one side. "Don't make it into a battle of wills. It's just what she wants."

"Then what can we do?"

She demonstrated. "Put her back down firmly and tuck her in tightly. She'll probably get up another time or two until it stops being fun. It's part of learning how to control your world and the people around you. Now she's worked out how to stand up she needs to know she can get down again on her own. All it takes is time.''

When they were seated at the dining table again with dessert in front of them he massaged his chin with one hand. ''With so many interruptions to their romance I wonder how parents ever get round to having more than one child.''

She laughed, the musical sound thrilling to his acoustically trained ears. ''They obviously find a way or the world would be full of only children.''

He refilled her wineglass and his own, then sat back, swirling the jewel-colored liquid so it caught the candlelight and fractured into diamond points. ''An only child would never do for me.''

She seemed to straighten, and her voice sounded off as she said, ''Why not?''

''After my mother left I found out the hard way how lonely it gets with only your own company.''

Her fingers whitened around the stem of her glass. ''You had your father and brother.''

''A father who shut himself off from the world and an older brother who soon went away to school, so I spent most of my time alone. It was only when I stayed with Aunt Edna and her brood that I felt truly alive. Then and there I promised myself I would have a big family like hers. Maree is going to have all the brothers and sisters I can give her.''

Bethany had pulled away from the light so he couldn't see her expression, but there was tension in every line of her slender body. ''And if you can't?''

''No risk there. My doctor assures me I check out perfectly on the baby-making scale, biologically I mean,'' he added with a grin. ''Modesty forbids me commenting on technique.''

''Of course.''

He didn't like the coldness he heard in her voice suddenly. "What is it?" he asked, since something was obviously wrong. "Aren't children important to you, too?"

She hesitated. "Isn't it a bit soon for us to be discussing children?"

"Probably, as long as I know the woman in my life wants them eventually. I didn't mean there's any hurry if that's what's worrying you." He leaned toward her. "You do want children of your own, don't you, Bethany?"

She lifted her head slowly. "Me? Good grief, no. I'm a career woman, remember? I have big plans for my publishing activities when I can afford them."

"And you intend your plans to come before having a family?"

She began to play with her dessert, not really eating it. "Naturally. Did you doubt it?"

He couldn't keep the disappointment out of his voice as he stood up and began to clear the table. "It was probably presumptuous of me, but as it happens, I did."

Chapter Six

Why had Nicholas chosen last night to bring up the subject of children? Bethany asked herself next morning. She was almost sorry she had the luxury of the morning to herself for once, because it left her too much time to think. Nicholas had taken Maree to the doctor for her regular checkup but had refused Bethany's offer to take her. He wasn't exactly cold toward her, but something had changed since last night, and she was afraid she knew exactly what it was.

He wanted children and he now believed Bethany didn't. She supposed they would have had to talk about it sooner or later, and it was probably just as well to get it over with. But she had been walking on air for most of yesterday evening and it had been a shock to be forced to come back to earth.

Kylie was also out, grocery shopping, so Bethany had the house to herself. She made coffee, being in no mood for breakfast, and carried it out onto the veranda to drink. Would it have helped to tell Nicholas the truth, that she wanted children more than anything in the world but she was unable to have them?

Then she remembered how Alexander had reacted when she told *him* the truth. She had made a promise never to put herself through such humiliation again. Pretending she was a career woman who didn't want anything standing in the way of her ambitions was surely less demeaning than leaving herself open to any more rejection.

She had reckoned without her growing feelings for Nicholas. She would have given anything not to have to see the disappointment in his eyes when she told him she didn't share his hopes for a large family. It was in cruel contrast to the way he had looked at her during the meal, as if she was a gift he had never thought he would receive.

Would he ever look at her that way again? It seemed unlikely, and even if he did, her conscience wouldn't let her encourage it, no matter how wonderful it felt. It was a no-win situation, she thought as a deep sigh was wrenched from her. If ever a man was cut out for fatherhood it was Nicholas Frakes. He deserved a woman who could share his dream. And Bethany deserved a man who would love her for herself. It made them as far from being soul mates as it was possible to get.

She started as the telephone rang, the sound amplified by an outside speaker so it could be heard around the vast gardens. It was unlikely to be for her, she thought as she got up to answer it. She had left Nicholas's number on her machine in Melbourne but so far most of her callers had chosen to leave messages for her to return.

"Except for brother Sam," he said cheerfully when she explained why she was surprised to hear from him. "I trust your boss isn't such a slave driver he objects to you getting personal calls?"

She laughed imagining Nicholas in such a role. "Hardly.

He took me bush walking yesterday, and today he's taken the baby for her checkup so I have the morning to myself.''

Sam whistled down the phone. "How do you get a job like that? I want to apply.''

"It helps to be good with babies,'' she said, knowing Sam would do almost anything to avoid being involved with infants.

"Guess that lets me out.'' There was a pause, then he said seriously, "I hate to be the bearer of bad news, but are you in some kind of trouble, little sister?''

"No, why?''

"I picked up your mail this morning and found a legal letter. You said I should open anything official, and this is so official I practically saluted it. It says if you don't pay your printer's bill within fourteen days, he'll see you in court, or words to that effect.''

Her throat went dry. "But he owes *me* money. He hasn't accounted for the deposit I gave him before he printed the last two issues of the journal.''

"Can you prove it?''

"He kept promising me a receipt, but I never received it.''

Sam gave a low moan. "First rule of business, get everything in writing, especially where money's concerned.''

"Just as well I have this job,'' she said soberly. "It sounds as if I'd better pay his bill before it gets any more complicated, then countersue him for my deposit.''

"Can you afford to pay him?''

This was a discussion she had hoped to avoid having with Sam. "Most of it,'' she said carefully. "Before you say anything, I don't want your money. You need it to run your own business and pay your employees.''

"I can afford to help you out,'' he told her, and overrode her objections with a growl. "Besides, I already sent him the check. I only called to let you know what was happening."

Tears prickled at the backs of her eyes. "Sam, you're impossible but I love you. Thank you. I'll pay you back in installments as soon as I can," she insisted.

"I know you will, even if I forbid it—heck, especially if I forbid it," Sam said cheerfully. "So pay me back when you're able." He took an audible breath. "Tell me, has your new boss proposed marriage yet?"

"I only work for Nicholas. He isn't about to propose anything," she denied, wondering if she wouldn't have been so certain yesterday. "He wants lots of kids and...well..."

"He doesn't know you can't have any?" Sam guessed. There were few secrets in the Dale family. Their joys and sorrows tended to be shared in equal measure. "A problem shared is a problem halved" was one of her mother's favorite expressions. Except that in this case it wasn't true. Bethany's sorrow wouldn't be halved, it would simply have another source.

Sam correctly interpreted her silence. "Not all men are the same. If you give him a chance, maybe Nicholas will surprise you."

If it was true, then she owed him her silence even more, she thought. "I'll think about it," she said with forced cheerfulness. Although he was probably aware of her tactic, Sam allowed her to change the subject to their family. She'd called her parents a couple of times since moving to Yarrawong, and Sam filled her in on the rest of the family news.

She felt less alone by the time they said their goodbyes and hung up. One of the joys of belonging to a large family was having support through thick and thin. It made her awareness of Nicholas's lonely teens even more poignant. Even if he was willing to accept her situation, she wasn't willing to cheat him of his chance at a real family life. It was the right decision. She only wished she felt happier about it.

He didn't seem all that happy, either, she noticed when he brought Maree home from the doctor. He looked grim as he slammed into the house and dropped his briefcase onto a chair with a crash. At first Bethany thought something must be wrong with the baby, but she looked radiant as she sat in her high chair, chewing on a piece of banana.

"She's perfectly healthy," he snapped. "The doctor says whatever we're doing we should keep doing it."

"For the baby," she said.

His pewter gaze searched her face. "Of course for the baby. We aren't doing anything else, are we?"

Last night she would have said they were close to putting their relationship onto a more personal footing. Today things were completely different. Since learning that she didn't want children he had built a wall around himself that she could barely see over. It was to be expected. By claiming to put her work ahead of everything else in her life, she had made him think she was ambitious and self-centered.

It wasn't a lovable picture, she had to admit, and it hurt to have him see her like that, but it served a purpose. As long as her supposed shallowness created an emotional chasm between them, he would never be forced to choose between her and his dream of a family.

"I guess Maree is all we have in common," she said flatly. "I enjoyed the bush walk yesterday and the dinner you prepared but—"

"But it was too cozily domestic to fit in with your plans for the future," he threw at her. "You made the point clear enough last night."

She laid a hand on his arm and felt an immediate surge of connection between them, so it was all she could do not to snatch her hand away. "Nicholas, I didn't mean to hurt you, but I can't change facts." The truth at last even if he didn't recognize it.

He looked at her hand as if something distinctly unappealing was crawling along his arm. "You didn't hurt me. You were right to let me know where you stand. But I would like to know one thing. If you're so determined not to let children interfere with your career plans, why are you here? Why aren't you working for some big-time publishing firm which can further your ambitions?"

She had no intentions of embroidering her lie. "Publishing jobs aren't easily come by."

"So taking care of Maree is purely a means of earning money?"

"Yes." She didn't trust herself to say more.

"Bull."

His explosive denial made her jump. "You don't believe me?"

"I don't believe you're the cold, calculating type to put a career ahead of a husband and family. You'd find a way to combine both. This dollhouse journal is supposedly your passion, yet you put it aside to work at a shelter for disadvantaged children, and you come up to the hills at the drop of a hat to take care of an orphaned baby. It doesn't add up."

As he faced her she felt her skin prickle with awareness of him. Even angry he looked magnificent, like a stallion at bay among the hills. He stood with his muscular legs wide apart, his tailored trousers strained by the aggressive stance so she couldn't help but be aware of his overwhelming masculinity. His palms were flat against narrow hips and there was a wildness in his expression, which alarmed her even as it sent surges of primal sensation along every vein in her body.

"Maybe it doesn't need to add up," she said huskily.

He shook his head. "I'm a scientist. You're a mystery, Bethany. Getting to the bottom of mysteries is *my* passion, one of them, anyway. You tell me one thing, but in my arms your body tells me another. One of you is lying."

The look on his face almost shattered her. He wanted answers and he wouldn't rest until he got them. If only she could give them to him. But it could only lead to two outcomes. Either he would insist that her childless state was no barrier to closeness between them or he would reject her out of hand. Knowing how much Nicholas wanted children she couldn't allow the first, and she wasn't sure if she could bear the second.

She tried to keep her body language from betraying her. If Nicholas suspected how much she had begun to care for him, he wouldn't rest until she admitted it. She managed to toss her head carelessly. "Can't I enjoy being kissed? It doesn't always have to mean something. Men do it all the time."

"This one doesn't."

The caution in his voice should have warned her, but she was unprepared when he pulled her into his arms. Resistance made her body stiff, but as soon as he touched her, a lump of pain in the center of her chest started to dissolve and she melted against him, her heart picking up speed. She had to fight to keep her true response from showing on her face.

Nicholas had no such problem. To him this was a scientific experiment to prove that his kiss engaged Bethany's deepest emotions. He wasn't letting her get away with the glib assurance that it was simply chemistry. She felt something for him, he would swear to it. He sure as blazes felt something for her. So why wouldn't she give it a chance to develop? She wanted him to write it off as mere lust, but he didn't buy it and he was sure she didn't, either. So what was going on here?

Few scientific experiments he'd conducted were so pleasant, he allowed as he set about getting her to open her mouth to him. His hands roved over her shirt, a thin woven affair through which he could feel her slight body trembling. Trembling meant she felt something, right? He slid his fingers down her spine, and she trembled again, adding a soft moan to the mix.

He took advantage of the moan to deepen the kiss, touching the tip of his tongue to hers in an experimental foray. Her eyes slid shut, and she tilted her head back, exposing the sweet column of her throat. He pressed his lips to it and felt the faint throb of a pulse. It became a flutter as he trailed kisses all the way to the inviting valley between her breasts.

"Nicholas, no, please."

Her fingers went to the buttons of her shirt which he'd started to unfasten. As he drew away from her she closed them again with shaking fingers. A mistiness in her eyes caught at him, slamming into him like a fist. Somehow he had managed to hurt her. It wasn't what he intended but he couldn't suppress a glimmer of satisfaction. If he could hurt her then he could heal her. She wasn't as immune to him as she pretended.

"Satisfied now?" she asked shakily.

"Are you?"

She turned away, her shoulders dropping so dejectedly that he couldn't help himself. He pulled her against his chest, feeling the hard knobs of her shoulder blades pressing against him. He kissed the top of her head lightly and felt her shudder. "It's all right, Bethany. I'm a louse. I shouldn't have done that."

She looked up at him over her shoulder. "I shouldn't have lumped you in with 'all men.' You aren't the type to kiss and run."

He settled his hands on her shoulders and turned her gently. "This isn't about me. It's about us."

She shook her head bleakly. "There isn't any us. There can't be."

"Why not? You said yourself there's no one waiting for you at home."

They were right back where they started. Only this time it hurt a lot more because Nicholas had done more than make his point. He had reminded her of what they could have shared if things had been different. "There's still my future and my plans for a career in publishing."

He swore softly and spun around. Lifting Maree from her high chair he swung her into his arms and left the room. Moments later she heard his footsteps on the cobblestones outside and the sound of the coach house door creaking open.

For a few minutes she remained in the center of the kitchen, trying to still the fast beating of her heart. Her tongue darted out to lick her lips. They felt full and bruised from the force of his kiss. She felt more vibrant than she could ever remember, as if his touch had brought every part of her to life. Something told her the memory of this moment would take a long time to fade, if it ever did.

It hadn't brought to life the one part of her that would make a difference, she thought, forcing back a choking sob. Nothing could change the fact that she couldn't give him his heart's desire. The only thing she could give him was freedom.

If she was going to convince him of her disinterest she would have to work much harder at it, she decided. No more half measures. He had to see her as a committed career person with big plans for the future. Otherwise he would keep trying to make her admit that she could care for him—and she was terrified that he might succeed.

Suiting the action to the thought, she went to her room

and searched through her things for a clipboard and pen and the camera she used to take photographs for the journal.

"Now we'll find out what sort of actor you'd make," she told her image in the mirror. She was alarmed at how pale she was beneath her light tan. Her teal blue eyes were ringed by violet shadows, but they lightened when she forced a grin at her reflection. The result was a bit bizarre but it was better than looking like Little Orphan Annie.

She was still practicing the grin when she let herself into the coach house but Nicholas didn't bother to look up from his computer. Maree was standing in the play area, her chubby fingers clenched around the bars of the safety fence. She gurgled a string of nonsense words, making the only greeting Bethany got.

It was what she wanted, she told herself. Still, nobody said she had to like it. "Do you mind if I take some photos and notes on the dollhouse now?" she asked Nicholas's unrelenting back.

He barely looked up. "Suit yourself."

"Thanks. I'm thinking of devoting a whole issue to it." But he was already back at work so she climbed the stairs to the loft, uncovered the magnificent dollhouse and started making notes. At any other time she would have considered it a privilege to spend as long as she wanted examining and photographing such a treasure, but part of her mind kept drifting to the man downstairs.

Of all the men in the universe, why did she have to be attracted to one with such a strong paternal instinct? To make matters worse, his easy affinity with Maree was one of his most beguiling features. Her insides twisted into knots every time she saw him cradle the little girl against the hard wall of his chest or rock her to sleep in his arms. Would Bethany want to wish that away if she could? It was sorely tempting to say yes but she knew it wasn't true. The mix of toughness and tenderness was what made him special.

A sigh whistled between her lips. It was also what made a future together impossible.

She closed the notebook with a thump. Her heart wasn't in the project right now. Maybe later when she'd had time to come to terms with her decision she could plan the article, but not yet. She reached for her camera. Nicholas would expect to hear her taking photographs so she may as well do so.

Two rolls of film later she had enough views of the house from all sides to illustrate several features. She took some close-up shots of individual pieces of furniture, then carefully replaced them in the house before closing it up and covering it again.

Nicholas was still at his desk when she went downstairs. "I have all I need for today, thank you," she said without expecting a response.

He turned to her. "I've been thinking. It isn't fair to expect you to stay here indefinitely when you have—other commitments. I have to go to Melbourne tomorrow to meet with the premier. While I'm in the city I'll see what I can do to find a replacement caretaker for Maree."

The coldness in his tone made her heart sink. Her performance with the dollhouse had been unnecessary. He had already bought the fiction that she was a career person with no interest in domesticity.

There was nothing she could say without contradicting her cover story so she nodded. "There's no hurry. I'm happy to stay until you find the right person."

"Thank you. I'll try not to detain you too long."

The air was so thick with his disapproval she could have cut it with a knife. He couldn't wait to be rid of her, she thought miserably. Reminding herself that she was doing the right thing for them both—the only thing she could do—was small consolation.

"Did you get everything you wanted upstairs?" he asked, his voice glacial.

"I still need to interview you about the house's history," she reminded him, finding herself contrarily pleased to have a reason to linger. "It can wait till you get back from Melbourne."

His answering look was ironic. "It will have to."

Before she could respond, the oak door creaked open and a stunningly beautiful woman walked in. "Your housekeeper told me I'd find you here, Nicholas."

The woman launched herself across the room and into Nicholas's arms, which came up reflexively to surround her. "Hello, Lana. What brings you here?"

Something cold and hard took root inside Bethany. This must be Lana Sinden, the model Nicholas had been seeing. She was every bit as gorgeous as her pictures in the magazines, with a glowing milky white skin and hair the color of buttermilk cascading in a satin curtain down her back.

Belatedly she noticed Bethany. "Who's this?"

"Lana Sinden meet Bethany Dale. Bethany has been taking care of Maree for me," he explained.

Lana's smile gleamed widely. "You finally found a nanny for the little pet. I must have sensed it when I decided to come back."

Nicholas frowned. "Bethany isn't a nanny. She's here as a favor to me."

Lana's finely pencilled eyebrows arched. "My apologies, Bethany. You must be doing a great job to keep Maree so—quiet." She winced a little at this but her smile was disarming. "You'll have to give me some pointers."

"Thinking of taking over Maree's care, Lana?" Nicholas sounded skeptical.

The model gave a slight shudder. "You know I'd be

useless at it.'' She shot Bethany a wary glance before turning to Nicholas. ''Can we talk privately?''

Bethany started for the door. ''I was going back to the house, anyway. Shall I take Maree with me?''

''Yes,'' Lana said.

''No,'' Nicholas said much more forcefully. ''You don't have to go, either, Bethany. Lana and I said everything we had to say before she packed up and left.''

''You mean you won't give me a chance to apologize?''

''I won't stop you. But you were right, country life and baby care aren't your thing. There's no need to apologize for being honest.''

Lana draped herself elegantly over the corner of Nicholas's desk. ''You're probably right. I did have some notion of starting over, but I can see you're as stubborn as ever.''

He sat back and folded his arms across his broad chest. ''Why did you come back, really?''

Lana's glance flickered to Bethany and back to Nicholas. ''To hold you to your promise to let *Spellbound* magazine do a photo spread here with me and Maree. They want to call it 'The Sexy Single Mother.'''

Bethany felt sick. It didn't even occur to Lana that Maree was a person, not a prop to be used to further her career. Nicholas evidently agreed because he shook his head. ''I won't go back on my word, although I gave it before you walked out, but I don't want Maree used in such a way.''

Lana looked pleadingly at him. ''I've already told them you'll agree. Surely you wouldn't make a liar out of me now, after all we've been to each other.''

''Don't tempt me.''

''I was there for you and the baby when she first came to you,'' Lana reminded him tautly. ''Staying up till all hours when she cried half the night.''

His mouth became a thin slash. ''I wasn't aware we were keeping score.''

"We're not, but you did promise, Nicholas. It won't take long, and Bethany can be there to make sure Maree is looked after."

It would probably suit Lana well to have Bethany on hand for any dirty work, she thought uncharitably. Then there was no chance the model would have to do it herself.

But Nicholas shook his head. "Maree isn't there to make you look decorative."

Lana frowned prettily. "But you won't stop me using Yarrawong as a background for some photos."

"What about the sexy single mother?" he asked ironically.

"They can change it to the sexy rural life, as long as they have me against a beautiful rural background," she amended. "I took you at your word and arranged everything."

Lana looked utterly crushed. All the same, Bethany was surprised when Nicholas relented. "Very well, I did promise, so you can take your photos here. But the crew is not to disturb Maree. I'm giving Bethany sole discretion to ensure they don't."

Lana looked relieved. "I wouldn't have it any other way." She leaned down and kissed Nicholas on the lips, her full mouth moving seductively over his. "Thank you, darling. What would I do without you?"

"Find someone else to wrap around your little finger," he muttered. But he didn't look too put out at being kissed by Lana. Bethany's own reaction caught her by surprise. For the first time in her life she understood the temptation to scratch another woman's eyes out.

It was hardly a defensible position, since she had disqualified herself as a lover for Nicholas, but it didn't stop a powerful wave of possessiveness from surging over her at the sight of Lana and Nicholas together.

"When does your crew want to come?" he asked, disentangling himself.

Lana smiled. "Tomorrow if it's convenient. We're working to a deadline."

"So am I. I'm meeting with the premier tomorrow in Melbourne."

Lana's smile faded. "I'll call the magazine and set another date."

"There's no need. You don't need me for your photographic session. I'd probably spend the time in my office and you wouldn't see me, anyway. Bethany is here to look after Maree. And you do know your way around the property, after all."

At the pointed reminder that the model had lived with Nicholas at Yarrawong until recently, Bethany felt her stomach lurch. She had no right to feel jealous, but she was afraid it was exactly what she did feel.

Nicholas turned to her. "I won't agree unless you're comfortable with this, Bethany."

Spending a day in Lana's company would remind Bethany of all she was giving up, but with Nicholas away, she couldn't abandon Maree to the model's care. "I'll manage," she said heavily. His look of gratitude warmed her far more than was wise. It didn't help to think of the favor as her parting gift to him.

Chapter Seven

"What's wrong, Bethany?" he asked her next morning over breakfast. "Won't you be in your element with Lana's people here? You could make some valuable contacts to boost your publishing career."

Some career person she was. The thought had never crossed her mind. Admitting it would undermine his belief in her plans she said, "You're right. It will be fascinating to watch the experts at work."

He drained his coffee cup and stood up. "Remember, you're in charge. Lana can be overpowering if she thinks she can get away with it."

At the reminder of how well he knew Lana, Bethany shivered. She couldn't believe he was as indifferent to the model as he appeared. Lana was the one who walked out, so perhaps this was his way of getting even.

"It's a pity you can't stay and watch her at work," she said, striving for fairness.

"I've had the privilege often enough to know it's a tedious business. Lots of standing around waiting, then a flurry of activity followed by more standing around. Not much fun for an onlooker.'' He moved closer, and her breathing quickened automatically. ''Although you'll no doubt enjoy yourself.''

He didn't know it but she mainly welcomed the photographic crew as a means of passing the hours until he got back. This would be the first time he'd been gone all day since she arrived, and already she felt lonely for him. Bethany couldn't help herself. Her eyes devoured him with the same enthusiasm Maree had shown for her breakfast.

His navy Armani suit managed to make his shoulders look broader and his body more hard muscled than usual. When he bent to replace a glass in a cupboard, the dark slacks stretched over his rear and she felt her knees weaken. Her breathing eased when he stood up, although watching him tuck his silk tie back into place was another exercise in self-control.

This would have to stop. Soon she would be back in Melbourne and he would be part of her past. The prospect was enough to make her feel physically ill.

He caught her arms. ''Hey, you've gone pale. Are you okay?''

Since her problem was a severe attack of imagining life without Nicholas, she couldn't very well tell him what was wrong. His touch made her heart flutter, but thankfully brought color back to her cheeks. ''I'm fine,'' she lied, twisting free of his hold. ''Isn't it time you got going?''

His features hardened as he misunderstood. ''Anxious to get me out of here so you can start the important business of the day?''

She turned away to hide her moist eyes. ''Say goodbye to Daddy, Maree.''

She lifted the child's tiny hand and Maree waved, making a sound that might or might not have been ''bye-bye.''

He kissed the child's downy head. ''Be a good girl for

Bethany.'' Picking up his briefcase he went to the door. ''Enjoy yourselves.''

''We'll see you off.''

On impulse she gathered Maree out of the high chair and followed him out to his car. He turned and waved, and she urged Maree to wave back. It was such a domestic scene that her throat caught. She could be his wife with their child in her arms, seeing her husband off to work. The beauty of the fantasy was almost overwhelming.

A wagon train of vehicles rolled into the clearing in front of the house, shattering the moment. Nicholas frowned as dust drifted over his Porsche, then frowned harder as Lana leaped from the lead car and threw herself at him.

''Darling, I'm glad you're still here. Come and meet the *Spellbound* crew.'' She towed Nicholas toward the cars disgorging people loaded with what looked like a ton of photographic equipment.

''Spellbound'' was right, Bethany decided, watching them cluster around Lana. Nicholas looked as if he would prefer to be on his way, but smiled and shook hands as he was introduced around. However, he didn't seem to object to Lana's arm linking with his as she drew him into her circle, Bethany noted.

She felt no need to join the introductions. Her job was to look after Maree and keep out of the way. She told herself it was what she was doing when she carried the baby back inside.

As Nicholas absently responded to Lana's introductions, he saw Bethany walk away and was waylaid by an urge to go after her, unable to shake the conviction that he had the wrong woman clinging to his arm. Lana was beautiful, he couldn't deny it. But she worked hard at her appearance while Bethany's appearance was entirely natural. What you saw was what you got.

Her looks were entirely unselfconscious, something he

could hardly say about Lana. Bethany didn't need perfect makeup or designer casual clothes to accentuate her beauty. That thing she was wearing, long and slinky with a patchwork skirt and black figure-hugging top, did such amazing things for her shape, he wished he could put the premier on hold for a few days and remain here.

The notion astonished him. Why didn't he feel the same way about Lana, who was the pinup of half the men in the country? Could it be because Lana would never put anything on hold for him?

He sighed. She was a lovely, sexy, desirable woman but she was also closed off to him in a way he hadn't understood until he'd met someone different. He had to admit that he knew more about Bethany after a few weeks than he knew about Lana after years. Oh, not the statistical stuff. Lana's was on file for the world to read. But what caused her joy or pain, what made her laugh or cry, whom did she count among her closest friends?

With Bethany he had a feeling that once she took you into her heart, you had a friend for life. What made Lana laugh or cry changed with prevailing fashions, and whom she thought of as a friend depended on expediency.

Take this crowd, for instance. Lana called them her friends and they treated her like royalty, but once the shoot ended they would transfer their loyalty to the next contender without a backward glance. It reminded Nicholas of when he had accompanied Lana to a guest appearance on a national television show. Lana had absorbed the star treatment beforehand—the limousines, the champagne and the flattery—like mother's milk. Then as soon as her spot ended it was as if she had ceased to exist. Bethany would never confuse such treatment with real friendship.

He already knew she was the kind to carry home stray animals or stray humans. He also knew only too well the fire in her response when he kissed her. He felt his mouth twist wryly as he remembered the feel of her supple body in his arms and the heat of her pliant lips against his own. Underneath the layers of Mother Teresa there was a goodly helping of Gypsy Rose Lee.

Lana tugged at his arm. "What are you smiling at? You're miles away."

He frowned and disengaged his arm. "It's where I should be by now."

She pouted prettily. "Can't you stay for a few hours. I work better when you're around to watch."

She worked better when everybody watched, he thought. "You'll be fine. You have the run of Yarrawong and Bethany will make sure the crew has everything they need."

"Everything except you," Lana persisted. "You didn't waste time replacing me with your little friend."

"She isn't little and she's nobody's replacement." Both were true. "Without Bethany's help with Maree I would never have finished this government project on time."

"She is on the chunky side, isn't she?" Lana heard only the first thing he said, the thing she wanted to hear. Compared to Lana's thinness, Bethany was more curvaceous, but for the life of him, he couldn't see it as a failing.

"Why is any woman with meat on her bones, chunky?" he demanded irritably. The more Lana forced him to compare the two women, the more he appreciated Bethany's special qualities, which was hardly Lana's intention. "There's such a thing as being too thin, you know."

The model lifted her arms in a graceful gesture. "You didn't say that when you used to hold me."

He may not have said it, but he had often thought it. "I was too distracted," he dissembled, knowing it would mollify her even if it wasn't the whole truth. Their relationship might be over, whether Lana accepted it or not, but it didn't mean he had to hurt her.

She practically purred. "I'm still good at distracting you, aren't I, darling?"

He welcomed the opening and nodded. "So it seems. I should have been on my way to Melbourne ten minutes ago."

As he intended, the implied compliment disarmed her long enough to let him take his leave and drive off, hoping he hadn't started something. But it wasn't the image of Lana which lingered in his mind as he gunned the powerful car down the old coach road toward the Calder Freeway. It was the thought of Bethany holding Maree in her arms and lifting the baby's tiny hand to wave goodbye to him that made him want to turn the car around.

Bleakness tore through him like an August wind. How could someone so wonderful with children be so set against having any of her own? It was the one flaw in a woman who attracted him as no other woman had ever done.

He didn't mind her wanting a career. He was perfectly willing to share the child-minding duties while his partner went out and did her thing, as long as they were both fulfilled and happy. But every vision he'd had of his future since he was eleven years old had included fatherhood. He wanted no part of a life as empty as the one he'd known as a boy. He refused to believe it was Bethany's choice of existence, either.

His palms slammed down on the steering wheel, and the car slewed until he fought it back under control. That was it! Bethany's insistence on having a career instead of a family didn't ring true. Combining the two would have made more sense than insisting she had no room in her life for children.

Was it only *his* children she didn't want? It was a real gut kicker of an idea, but he forced himself to consider it fairly. Maybe his genes simply didn't appeal to her. He'd heard of women shopping for suitable father material. Was she one of them? It seemed so unlike the Bethany he knew that he dismissed it out of hand. If he had repelled her to that extent she wouldn't have all but melted in his arms.

He had a feeling the puzzle was going to nag at him all the way to Melbourne and back.

Some women had everything—beauty, a business brain and an ability to charm the birds from the trees, Bethany thought as she carried Maree into the house. The image of Nicholas and Lana together persisted in her mind. No doubt she was also as fertile as a rabbit. Last year one of the scandal sheets had written about Lana supposedly having given a baby up for adoption in her teens. It was probably a fairy tale, since Lana had denied it strenuously. Nothing more had been heard of the supposed love child after that one story.

Was she being unfair? Bethany asked herself. Jealousy wasn't usually one of her vices and famous people were always targets for scandal. But the very thought of any woman bearing a child she didn't want was like salt in Bethany's emotional wounds. It seemed every other woman took for granted what she would give her soul to produce.

She decided to make amends for her lack of charity by being extra nice to the crew while they worked. Kylie had taken the day off to visit her grandmother but had left plenty of food prepared so Bethany provided a steady stream of coffee, cake and sandwiches.

"These are great, thanks," the lighting man said, around a mouthful of homemade muffin. "We don't usually get service like this from the people we visit." He looked around. "This place is beautiful. Have you lived here long?"

"I only work here. It belongs to Dr. Nicholas Frakes."

The man's eyes gleamed. "Isn't he Lana's ex? Now I know why she put this project together in such a hurry."

Bethany felt a frown etch her forehead. "Aren't you doing a spread for *Spellbound* magazine?"

"That's the general idea. But we were hired by Lana, not the magazine. She got them interested, but they want to see the pictures before committing themselves."

It wasn't the story Lana had told Nicholas. He might not have been so easily persuaded if he had known the feature was purely speculative. It also explained Lana's disappointment at his absence which put to rest any hopes she had of using the day to patch up the relationship. Not that their love life was any business of hers, Bethany told herself grimly, almost believing it.

Finally tiring of providing Lana with an audience, she asked if anyone needed anything before she took Maree inside. She could put her time to better use by working on her dollhouse article while Maree napped.

"Do you have to go in now?" Lana asked. "Nicholas tells me you publish a specialist magazine. You should talk to Grayden Nichols. He knows everyone in the business and could open doors for you."

Grayden was the photographer masterminding the shoot. Bethany nodded. "I've seen his byline in dozens of magazines. But I'm not planning a career in publishing."

Lana's eyes narrowed. "What are you planning a career in?" She looked at the baby bouncing on Bethany's hip. "It wouldn't be motherhood, by any chance?"

Her love life was no business of Lana's either. "You never know."

"You mean you actually like changing babies and mopping goo off their faces?"

"Somebody has to, or none of us would make it to adulthood."

Lana shuddered delicately. "I'm sure I was never as messy as this kid."

"Maree isn't as messy as some," Bethany said, thinking

of some of the infants she'd cared for at the shelter. "She's a pleasure to look after—aren't you, sweetheart?"

Maree tugged at a locket around Bethany's neck and she tilted her head back, removing the bauble from harm's way. Maree reached for it. "Ah, ah, ah."

There was a binding flash and a triumphant cry of "got it" before Grayden Nichols joined them, camera in hand.

Maree looked bemused by the flash then reached for the camera. She made protesting noises when it was also removed from her grasp. Bethany thrust a bunch of plastic keys into the baby's fist and jiggled them to distract her as she regarded the photographer with dismay. "Tell me you didn't take my picture? I look a sight."

In contrast to Lana's gorgeous lapis lazuli Aloys Gada pantsuit and flowing silk scarf, Bethany felt drab. Her dress had a knitted top to hug her curves and a flowing patchwork skirt to flatter the bits which were better not hugged too tightly. It was a longtime favorite but had definitely seen better days. Her hair was also a froth of tangled curls thanks to Maree pulling it.

Grayden grinned. "You look fresh and natural. Too cute to miss."

Lana's smile didn't reach her eyes. "A regular Madonna and Child." Then she brightened. "But it reminds me. I promised Nicholas we'd take a few shots of me with Maree—for Nicholas's scrapbook," she added as Bethany opened her mouth to protest.

She could hardly refuse to let Lana pose with the baby if they were for Nicholas himself. He had vetoed the idea for publication but he may well have agreed for his own use, making the arrangements when Lana arrived this morning. The two of them had talked for long enough before Nicholas left for Melbourne. All the same Bethany felt uneasy as the model lifted Maree from her arms.

Maree wasn't impressed, either. As soon as the strange

arms closed around her she stiffened all her limbs and gave
a strangled cry. Hefting her in one arm, Lana tried to pat
her with the other, as if she was a puppy. ''There, there.
Be good for Auntie Lana while we take your picture.''

Taking pity on the model who was hopelessly out of her
depth, Bethany jiggled the toy keys in front of Maree who
stopped wailing and made a grab for them. They were im-
mediately transferred to her mouth.

Lana made the mistake of trying to remove them. ''Not
in your mouth, kid. It's not a good look. Now smile for the
nice man.''

Maree snatched the keys back but they dropped to the
ground and she started to struggle hard, wanting only to
follow her toy down to the ground. Lana gave a grunt as a
small foot connected with her midsection. ''This little thing
has a kick like Steven Seagal. Can't you make her stay still
for two minutes, Bethany?''

''Not if she doesn't want to cooperate. Does it matter for
a family album?'' Why didn't Grayden Nichols take the
pictures and get it over with?

Lana shot her an icy look. ''I have a reputation to think
of. Can't you do something to calm her down? I'm sure
she's hyperactive or something.''

''I can give her the nap she's overdue for,'' Bethany said
through clenched teeth. If this went on much longer she
was taking the baby inside, Nicholas or no Nicholas.

Luckily Maree decided to settle down, for the moment
at least. Lana looked at the baby's floppy sun hat before
lifting it off and dropping it on the ground, frowning in
distaste. ''Don't they sell designer baby wear in the Central
Highlands?''

Bethany started to point out that protecting a baby's delicate skin from the sun was more important than having
her look fashionable, but Lana was out of earshot. Picking
up the discarded hat Bethany hastily followed the pair.

Lana carried Maree to where a grove of tree ferns made a scenic backdrop. "How do I look?"

"Fantastic, a picture of maternal beauty," Grayden muttered, working his camera furiously. He gestured to the lighting assistant who unfurled a silver umbrella and angled it to shine more light onto Lana's stunning features. The action intrigued Maree who stopped protesting and stared in fascination at the umbrella.

"Great, turn her toward me a little more. That's it. Beautiful," the photographer chanted, snapping steadily. He waved an arm above his head and Maree followed it with her eyes. This was better. Lots of attention and new moving things to watch.

The photographer glanced over his shoulder toward Bethany. "The magazine is going to flip over these shots. The kid's a natural."

Without thinking, Bethany interposed herself between the cameraman and his subjects. "The magazine won't be seeing these photos. You said they're for Nicholas," she accused Lana. "Maree is not a performing seal."

"Can't you see she loves the attention?" Lana asserted. "In any case she's practically my child, or she will be as soon as Nicholas and I get back together."

Lana's matter-of-fact manner was more convincing than if she'd indulged in histrionics. Bethany's heart turned leaden in her chest and her breathing felt strangled, but she fought for control. "Your plans are between you and Nicholas. He left Maree in my charge today, and I don't want her posing for any more photographs."

Bethany reached for the baby but Lana's hold tightened. "We only need a few more shots. Grayden is almost finished here."

As far as Bethany was concerned he *was* finished. Maree started to wail despairingly, making it clear she'd had more than enough of Lana. Which made two of them, Bethany thought, tight-lipped. Nicholas might have warned her that he and Lana meant to patch things up. It put Bethany in the awkward position of interfering between the baby and the woman who might soon become her mother.

A woman who should have more compassion for a child's distress, she reminded herself, angrily replacing the sun hat on Maree's downy head. Bethany hoisted the child onto one hip and dried her tears, jiggling her up and down and crooning until she began to chortle. "Better, sweetheart?"

"Ah, ah, ah."

She became aware of Lana's intrigued looked and made herself say, "Would you like to hold her? Not for the camera, just to make friends?"

Lana sniffed the air. "No, thanks. I think she needs changing or something. This outfit's only on loan. I can't risk ruining it," she added when Bethany was unable to hide her disapproval.

Bethany nodded. "I'll take her back to the house." On the way she turned, curiosity getting the better of her. "How will you manage when her brothers and sisters come along?"

Lana pretended to fan herself. "Don't say such dreadful things even in jest. I don't intend to risk my figure having any of my own. One like Maree is more than enough, thanks."

Not enough for Nicholas, Bethany thought as she went back inside. She remembered his reaction only too well when she told him she didn't want children. It had spelled the end of any chance of a future between them. But it was better than facing his inevitable rejection once he knew the truth, she told herself. In Lana's case it was a free choice but one Bethany would never accept.

Bethany found it hard to stop her spirits from rising as she changed the baby and organized a snack for her. Whoever Nicholas married it wasn't going to be Lana Sinden. The reconciliation was probably wishful thinking, too.

The knowledge buoyed her up while the camera crew repacked their gear and stowed it into the convoy of cars. Lana looked as if she would like to linger until Nicholas returned but Grayden Nichols was impatient. "Time is money, sweetness," he reminded her. "If we stay any longer we'll be on golden time."

"They only pay that sort of overtime in films," Lana snapped back. But she got into the passenger side of Grayden's car and wound down the window, leaning toward Bethany. "Tell Nicholas I'll call him tonight about our plans."

"I'll tell him," Bethany said. A couple of hours before, the promise would have galled her. Now her emotions were tangled. She knew Lana wasn't the right woman for Nicholas, so there was no point distressing herself with jealous imaginings. Knowing Lana had no future with him, she used the thought to lift her tattered spirits.

"You're in a much happier mood than when I left," Nicholas said a short time later as he came into the kitchen and tossed his briefcase onto a handy chair. The strain of the day showed in the tightness around his eyes, but he looked so virile that her heart skipped a beat.

"It's because the magazine people have gone," she blurted out, then bit her lip. He might not love Lana but it didn't mean he would appreciate Bethany criticizing her.

Instead he laughed. "Tough day, I gather?"

"Now I know how Cinderella felt waiting on the ugly stepsisters."

He frowned. "Fetching and carrying for the crew wasn't your job."

"I wanted to help." She didn't add it was to make amends for her lack of charitable thoughts toward Lana when she first arrived.

"Working with the magazine crew must make baby minding seem humdrum by comparison."

She weighed her response with care. If she denied it, she undermined her image as a dedicated career person. Yet it wasn't in her to agree. "Looking after a baby is never humdrum," she assured him. "Maree loved being in front of the camera, at least until the novelty wore off."

His pewter eyes narrowed. "She what? I left instructions she was not to be used in the photographs. I relied on you to make sure she wasn't."

His censure stung. "Now just a minute. According to Lana, the pictures of her and Maree were for your family album."

Some of his anger subsided but a glint remained in the look he turned on her. "Were they now? It never occurred to you that Lana might lie to get her own way? It wouldn't be the first time."

"As it happens it did occur to me, but I could hardly say so in front of the crew, in case you had authorized the pictures. I allowed Maree to pose only for a few minutes before I rescued her."

She was tempted to tell him about Lana's certainty that she would soon be Maree's foster mother. She felt sure it was another fantasy, but it would reveal how much the question interested Bethany, which was the last thing she wanted him to know.

He dropped into the armchair beside the fireplace and flexed his hands behind his head. "Sounds as if you handled Lana pretty well."

"Thank you," she said primly, but felt vindicated. "Maree is bathed, fed, changed and fast asleep now."

"Tired out by all the excitement," he assumed. He rubbed his eyes. "I know exactly how she feels."

Instantly her heart went out to him. "How was your meeting?"

He grimaced. "The premier knows what he wants, but the rest of the committee he appointed to oversee the security project need to brush up on their technology. Most of them still think it's enough to sweep a room for listening devices before holding a top-level meeting. They got a shock when I explained all the ways you can eavesdrop on their activities from a block away."

He stood up and stretched. "But it created a good climate for my proposals, which were accepted in their entirety."

Her pleasure was unrestrained. "Congratulations. All your hard work paid off."

"It wasn't the only progress I made while I was in Melbourne, Bethany."

An edge in his voice made her look up. "What do you mean?"

"I also found out why you're so anxious to keep some distance between us."

Chapter Eight

A chill swept through her in spite of the evening warmth. She wrapped her arms around herself protectively. How on earth had he managed to discover that she couldn't have children? She had no doubt that it spelled the end of any closeness between them.

So she was unprepared when he said, "It's because of your uncle, isn't it?"

Stupidly she stared back at him. "Excuse me?"

He came closer and her heart rate jumped. "I sensed you were keeping something from me, and guessed it involved the dollhouse. So I visited one of my mother's distant relatives who lives in a retirement village in Melbourne and pumped him for information. He was surprised to hear from me after all this time, and his memory isn't too reliable, but he remembered enough for me to put the pieces together."

"The pieces of what? Nicholas, I have no idea what this is about."

He took her gently in his arms and pulled her closer.

"You can stop pretending now, Bethany. I know the man my mother ran away with was your uncle."

She felt light-headed with confusion, not least because she was in his arms again. She wished there was a graceful way to extricate herself. It would be easier to think straight without his hands resting on her shoulders, his mint sweet breath caressing her cheek. "My uncle? Are you serious?"

He tilted her chin up with one hand, his eyes searching hers. "My Lord, you didn't know, did you?"

"I knew Uncle Seth got married and went to live overseas, but I never met his wife. I gathered there was a scandal involved because my family didn't talk about it much. I was a child when he left. He was the one who told me about the Frakes Baby House."

"And you never wondered how he knew so much about this particular dollhouse?"

"He was a craftsman who made me my first dollhouse, so I knew they were a hobby. I guess I thought it was the reason for his interest. When he spoke about the Frakes Baby House he made it sound so wonderful that I promised myself I would see it when I grew up. I never asked why he found it so interesting."

Nicholas's expression hardened. "The house brought him to Yarrawong, but it wasn't what made him keep coming back. He must have begun his affair with my mother almost from his first visit. He's your mother's brother, isn't he?"

She nodded. "His name is Seth Baker."

A shadow darkened his features. "Under the circumstances, I'll never forget his name, although I didn't know anything about the man himself. My mother's relative remembered enough about the affair to give me a few leads so I was able to establish his relationship to you. Because his surname was different from yours, I had no reason to connect him with you when we first met."

She felt his anger as a living vibration traveling through her body which reacted like a tuning fork to his touch. Her voice dropped to a whisper. "I'm so sorry, Nicholas. I swear I had no idea."

His look intensified. "You can't think I blame you for his actions? You weren't responsible any more than I was. If anyone's at fault it was my father for neglecting his marriage and creating a climate where my mother felt driven to seek love from another man." Nicholas brushed the hair back from her face with one hand, letting his fingers linger in the soft curls. "I thought once I told you I'd found out, it would make things better between us. But nothing's changed, has it?"

She took a step back, missing the warmth of his embrace almost as soon as the gulf widened between them. She was shaken by his discovery but, in a way, relieved. She had loved Uncle Seth and felt betrayed when he left to live overseas. Now she understood why he and his new bride had been compelled to begin a new life elsewhere.

She was glad Nicholas didn't hold it against her, but it wasn't the secret she was keeping from him, so nothing had really changed. If only it was the problem, everything would have been solved. But by being so understanding Nicholas had actually made it harder for her to walk away.

"I'm glad you told me," she said quietly.

"But it doesn't help, does it?" he anticipated, coldness sharpening his tone. The darkness in his eyes told her he'd been counting on the news to perform a miracle between them. A miracle is what it would take for her to decide to stay.

For one brief moment she wondered if she was being fair to him. He had talked about his love of children and his dream of a large family without knowing her situation. If he knew, he might be willing to give up his plans in exchange for a future together.

She hugged herself. It was precisely why she wasn't pre-pared to tell him. The thought of Nicholas rejecting her was beyond contemplating. Worse still would be his will-ingness to understand, to sacrifice his dream for her. She couldn't allow him to do it.

Her smile felt fixed. "I explained my reasons for wanting to return to Melbourne. They haven't changed."

The silence deepened, then he fished in his briefcase and pulled out a sheaf of papers so old they were the color of parchment and almost as brittle. "Then it's just as well I brought these for you."

She took the papers from his hand, and their fingers brushed, igniting the familiar flare of awareness deep inside her at his touch. Focusing on the papers helped her to fight temptation. "What are they?"

His look reflected her sudden leap of desire as if he would also like to sweep the papers aside and take her into his arms. Her stomach tightened in anticipation but he said, "They're the plans to the Frakes Baby House. My legal adviser had them filed among the family papers."

Instead of fueling her elation, his generosity made her feel worse. "These are the original plans. They must be valuable."

"They're on loan for as long as you need them." He cleared his throat. "If you offer copies to your readers as a premium, it should lift circulation somewhat."

She gasped. "Somewhat? Have you any idea of what a find like this would mean to a serious collector of minia-tures?"

He gave a cynical smile. "I'm glad I finally found a way to get you excited."

If he only knew, he had done that almost from the mo-ment they met. His offer wasn't nearly as breathtaking as his closeness. She was enveloped in the lingering aura of his expensive aftershave lotion, and his suit sleeve brushed her arm. With her heightened sensitivity she could have described the fabric by touch alone. One turn was all it would take to bring them together. She made herself think about the plans. "It's a generous offer, but I can't accept."

His impatient breath whistled between them. "Why on earth not? It's what you want, isn't it, a way to make your journal into a big success?"

"It is what I want," she agreed because he expected it. The truth couldn't be more different. "But not this way."

His mouth became a hard slash. "Because you don't want anything more to do with me?"

"Good grief, no." It was out before she could stop herself. The answering gleam in his eyes was almost her undoing until she dragged in a deep breath to resist the surge of pure physical sensation clawing at her. "I mean I'm thrilled to have the chance to publish the original plans to the dollhouse, but won't it create too much interest in the house? I thought you didn't want enthusiasts beating a path to your door."

"I can cope. I'm a big boy," he reminded her dryly.

Of all the ways he could have phrased it, did he have to choose the one guaranteed to send her imagination into overdrive? In her sensitized state, his size and masculinity were his two qualities least in doubt. "You'd risk having hordes of collectors besieging your home, to help me?"

He frowned. "One of us has to get our priorities straight. I care about you, and if the way to demonstrate it is to drag that blasted dollhouse back into the spotlight, then I'm willing to do it."

How far was she willing to go on his account, was the implied question. To the end of the earth and back, was the answer. She was already doing it, but her success depended on him not knowing the extent of her sacrifice. She affected a careless shrug, although her heart felt as if it was being squeezed in a vise. "Then I can't refuse such a generous offer although I don't know how I can ever thank you."

He gave her a measured look. "I can think of a way."

So could she, and alarm shrilled through her at the thought of kissing him again. Since he got home she had endured the sweet torment of imagining his arms around her as she pressed herself against him and the sensual heat of his body radiated through her. It had taken every ounce of restraint she possessed to maintain her distance. Even a simple thank-you kiss would be playing with fire.

There was only one way she could keep from revealing how deeply she had started to care for him. Kiss him as if it meant nothing more than appreciation of his generosity. She pulled in a steadying breath, raised herself on tiptoe and pressed her lips against his cheek. Or it would have been his cheek if he hadn't turned his head at the last moment.

Instantly what should have been a chaste peck, over in seconds, turned into a lingering exploration of her lips. Desire flamed to the depths of her being. Almost without conscious thought she slid her hands up and linked them around his neck.

The gesture pulled his head down, and he nuzzled the side of her neck, nipping teasingly at her earlobe until the room temperature started to climb. Her clothes suddenly felt constricting and her heart rate soared.

"It's hot in here," she protested weakly, fairly sure that the weather had nothing to do with the heat wave pouring through her.

His fingers tangled in her hair. "I could arrange for it to get a lot hotter. You know I want you, Bethany. And no matter how you try to disguise it, I'm positive you feel the same way."

So much for keeping secrets from him, she thought despairingly. She should have known that kissing him for any reason was flirting with danger. With Nicholas there were no chaste kisses. They were the kind to get a woman well and truly caught, something she couldn't allow for both their sakes.

She started to wriggle free, which was another mistake. It brought her body into closer contact with his and she felt her face flame at the realization of how ready he was to turn up the heat between them.

An old maxim leaped into her mind—if you can't stand the heat, get out of the kitchen. That's what she had to do, get out of the kitchen before her remaining resolve went up in smoke. She flattened her palms against the thickly padded muscle of his shoulders. "Nicholas, we have to stop this."

His mouth moved provocatively against her hairline but he pulled back a little and searched her face. "Why? We're both free and well past the age of consent. If you're worried about all those babies I told you I wanted, there's no hurry. I'll make sure you're protected until we both agree the time is right."

His promise was meant to reassure her, but unknowingly, he plunged her into the depths of despair. She couldn't deny she wanted him, but he had just restated the overwhelming reason why giving in to it would be a mistake.

Get out of the kitchen, she reminded herself. She pushed herself free, aware of the tousled state of her hair and clothing and her rushed breathing. "I'm sorry, Nicholas." There was nothing more she could think to say.

He let her go, and his arms dropped to his sides but his fingers curled into fists. "The time will never be right for you and me, will it, Bethany?"

"It's better this way," she said miserably.

"Because of your commitment to your work?" She nodded and he made a furious sound of denial. "Since when does having a career require a vow of celibacy? The world is full of two-career families."

Family being the operative word where he was concerned. She was saved from having to respond by Maree crying, the sound of her babyish distress amplified through the intercom that connected the other rooms with her bedroom.

Bethany thrust a hand through her hair, lifting it from her scalp, which tingled where his fingers had wandered through it. "I'd better go to her."

"I'll come with you."

Why couldn't he let her make a graceful exit? Thanks to the last few minutes she felt overheated and very, very aroused. She was achingly aware of him as he followed her down the vaulted hallway to the bedroom that had been made into a light, airy nursery for Maree. Nicholas's brother and sister-in-law had decorated it in anticipation of the baby's arrival, Nicholas had told her.

As a result the decor reflected their love and commitment to their child, with glossy white furniture in the Federation style, and hand-painted murals decorating the walls. On the high ceiling was a painted blue sky speckled with fluffy white clouds. The room was practically a shrine to all the reasons why Bethany could never belong here.

Her own concerns were pushed aside as soon as she touched the baby. "She's burning with fever."

He slid in beside her and touched the back of his hand to Maree's forehead. "You're right. Stay with her while I get a thermometer."

He was back in minutes, but they seemed like hours as Bethany cradled the distressed child in her arms. Maree's face was flushed, although her skin felt dry. Her pulse raced and her breathing sounded labored.

When Nicholas checked the child's temperature it was several degrees above normal. Bethany began to remove

Maree's clothes. "Get me something wet to wrap her in, a sheet or a towel."

When he brought it, she swathed the baby in the damp folds then asked him to turn on a ceiling fan to direct cooling air over Maree's fevered body.

He did as she asked. "What's the matter with her?"

"I'm not a nurse, but it looks like she got too much sun today. As soon as we get her temperature down we should take her to the hospital."

"How in blazes could this happen?"

She winced, knowing he wouldn't like the answer. "The only time she was exposed to the sun was while Lana insisted on having them pose together." She turned agonized eyes to him. "It's my fault for letting them use Maree in their pictures."

He shook his head. "It isn't your fault. I should know Lana well enough by now. Wild horses can't shift her once she gets an idea into her head. If anyone's to blame it's me for letting her through the front gate. I can guarantee it won't happen again." He caressed the top of the baby's damp head. "Is it wishful thinking or does she feel a little cooler already?"

Bethany checked the baby's temperature again. "Her temperature is down a little. It should be safe to drive her to the hospital now."

He didn't waste time. "I'll bring the car around to the front door. You throw whatever she'll need into a bag and meet me there."

It didn't take long to get ready. As an afterthought Bethany added a few things she and Nicholas might need if there was a long wait at the hospital while Maree was checked over. Bethany's sense of alarm was rapidly diminishing as the baby's color improved and her breathing quieted, but it was better to be safe than sorry.

"You're too precious to risk, aren't you, little one?" she

murmured as she carried the baby and the bag out of the house. Nicholas strapped Maree into the safety seat and readily agreed when Bethany offered to ride in the back with her.

Nicholas was shaken by the incident, she saw from the tense set of his shoulders and the grim way he gripped the steering wheel. "Is this her first real illness?" she asked him.

In the driving mirror she saw him nod. "I was warned that babies go through all kinds of ailments."

"And most survive them all," she said firmly.

He remained unconvinced until a doctor had examined Maree and confirmed a mild case of heat stroke. "You did all the right things," he assured Bethany. "Have you had some experience nursing children?"

She nodded. "I'm an aide at the Infants' Shelter in Melbourne."

The young doctor smiled and again complimented her on her first aid skills.

"There was no real need to keep Maree here overnight. Young Doctor Sideburns said she's fine now her temperature is back to normal," Nicholas snapped when they returned to the waiting room after the baby was admitted to the children's ward for observation.

She regarded him curiously. "He's only being cautious."

His face was cold and shuttered. "He was coming on to you."

It was extraordinary how elated his obvious jealousy made Bethany feel. She pushed the sensation away. "All the same, he did the right thing. By morning we'll be sure nothing else caused her rise in temperature." She stretched languorously. "Just what I need after today, a night spent in a hospital waiting room." By mutual consent they had agreed to stay in town overnight, ready to take Maree home as early as they could next morning.

"We don't have to stay in the waiting room. There's a hotel across the road, and their Vacancy sign was still up when we arrived."

She groaned aloud. "I can't afford a hotel room. I'm broke." On that morning she had sent her brother the first instalment on her printer's bill.

"My treat," he insisted. When she started to argue, he silenced her with a shake of his head. "You were wonderful with Maree. It's the least I can do to repay you."

"But you're already paying me to take care of her." In truth it was the prospect of spending a night at a hotel with him that shook her to her core. In his arms tonight she had barely managed to resist temptation. In a hotel, without the responsibility of the baby, she wasn't sure she could keep saying no to him.

"Then consider it a fringe benefit." He picked up the overnight bag she'd packed in haste and steered her toward the door.

The hotel did indeed have a vacancy but there was a problem. At this late hour there was only one room available. "We'll take it," Nicholas stated without looking at her.

She had been aware of his growing tension in the hospital. Now she saw his hand shake as he signed the register. Concern for him overrode her misgivings about sharing a room.

"What is it, Nicholas? What's the matter?" she asked when they were finally alone. The room wasn't large, and it took a determined effort not to fix her gaze on the queen-size bed which was the only sleeping accommodation.

He went to the bar and poured himself a scotch with a splash of iced water. "Drink?" he queried, his voice deeper and huskier than she had ever heard it.

"No, thank you. I'm more worried about you." Then

light dawned. "It's Maree, isn't it? It was just one of those baby things. She'll be fine by morning, you know."

He downed the drink in one toss. "I know it now."

"Then what is it? Something's bothering you. Your hands are shaking."

He looked down at them as if seeing them for the first time. She could see the effort of will he exerted to steady them but the faintest tremor remained. He dragged in a deep breath. "Tonight, I thought I might lose Maree," he grated, closing his eyes.

Her heart turned over. He had lost a brother and feared he was going to lose a niece as well. Without thinking she crossed the room and put her arms around him, resting her head against his shoulder. His body was rigid with tension and she felt his pain as if it was her own. "Maree is going to be fine. Would a good-looking young doctor lie to a woman he's hoping to date?"

As she'd intended her teasing tone pierced the armor of his memory and he cracked a slight grin. "Shows how much you know about good-looking young doctors."

"Fine, upstanding pillars of the community," she continued in the same deliberately light tone.

"Who would lie through their teeth to get you to go out with them," he added. "I ought to know. I was one, once."

She tilted her head to regard him quizzically. "Which were you—good-looking, young or a doctor?"

He pretended indignation. "I was young once, and I was a premed student before I switched to acoustical engineering."

"And you are still good-looking," she assured him, her voice breaking slightly on the compliment. She pictured him as a handsome young doctoral candidate, so intense and committed to his research he never knew he was leaving a trail of broken hearts behind him. "Does this mean you're lying through your teeth to get me into bed with you?''

His gaze raked her face as if he was committing her features to memory. ''I have never lied to you, Bethany, and I never will.''

She felt the heat roll up her face. ''I was joking. But I'm glad to see you're feeling better.''

His arms tightened around her. ''I'll show you how much better I'm feeling.'' Before she had time to react, he slid an arm under her knees and hoisted her against his chest. Then he carried her across the room and deposited her on the bed.

She struggled against the wash of movement in the too-soft mattress and managed to sit up. Her gesture of comfort seemed to be rebounding with a vengeance. ''This wasn't what I had in mind.''

He loomed over her, his grin reminding her of her brother Sam in one of his more devilish moods. ''And it isn't why I brought you here. Relax, the bed's yours. I'll sleep on the chair and use the coffee table as a footstool.''

She didn't know whether to feel relieved or disappointed. Rather more of the latter she suspected. She mentally measured his six-foot length against the chair, which was designed more for show than for comfort. ''You'll do no such thing. The bed's wide enough for two.''

''I'm not sure it's a good idea.''

Neither was she, but it wasn't fair to condemn him to a sleepless night in a chair because she couldn't control her hormones. She swallowed around a lump that filled her throat. ''You said yourself, you're a big boy. Surely we can be grown-up about this?''

His look was darkly assessing. ''That's what worries me. You're way too grown-up to share a bed with a man platonically.''

''So you're afraid you can't control yourself?'' A well

of pleasure surged through her at the prospect of driving him to the brink of self-control.

He looked offended. "I can control myself as well as the next man."

Her heart was racing a mile a minute, but she managed a calm smile. "I know I can control myself, so what's the problem?"

He shook his head in pained disbelief. "You obviously haven't looked in a mirror lately."

"So we're back to me."

He growled in exasperation. "Why are we even having this discussion? Frankly, I'm too tired to be any use to you anyway, so move over. I sleep on the right side."

She scrambled off the bed long enough to retrieve a T-shirt from the bag. She hadn't intended it as night attire, but had thought she might welcome a change of clothes if she had to sit up all night at the hospital.

By the time she returned from the bathroom wearing the T-shirt and carrying her clothes, Nicholas was in bed. Only then it occurred to her that she hadn't packed anything suitable for him to sleep in. So what was he wearing under the covers?

From where she stood it didn't look as if he was wearing anything. He lay with one arm crooked under his head and a blanket pulled up to his waist. The sight of such a broad expanse of bare chest was almost her undoing. Her glance flickered to the armchair. Perhaps it would be wiser if she slept there after all. Nicholas might be sure of maintaining control, but around him Bethany was no longer certain about her own ability.

He seemed to read her mind. "Don't even think about it. There's plenty of room in this bed."

That was before he got into it. Now her side looked alarmingly narrow. It wasn't that Nicholas was greedy. There was just so much of him. She swallowed hard. "I

brought a book along. I...I might read for a while befor
turning in.''

His lazy grin told her he wasn't fooled. "Do I have t
get up and put you to bed myself."

The thought of being tucked in by Nicholas triggered a
attack of butterflies inside her. Only these weren't butter
flies. They were F-111 fighter jets. "All right, I'm com
ing," she yelped and scooted around to the left-hand sid
of the bed. To emphasize his threat, he had reared up fa
enough to confirm her worst fears. He wasn't wearing any
thing at all.

Her heart slammed against her ribs as she slid betwee
the sheets, inching her way across the bed, every sense aler
for the first touch of skin to skin. She felt as if she wa
ready to jump out of hers. This was a bad idea. A very ba
idea. Nicholas had a unique ability to inflame her sense
beyond all reason. Yet, she could never be the kind of wif
he wanted. So she was playing with fire going anywher
near him after sundown, far less getting into a bed wit
him in a hotel room where there was no baby intercom
nothing to interrupt whatever happened next.

"Do you always sleep at attention?" he asked dryly.

Only when she was trying to balance on the very edg
of a soft mattress which threatened to roll them togethe
into the middle, she thought. "I'm a little tense," she ad
mitted. It had to be the understatement of the year.

He sat up and the covers slid down, further revealing
more golden skin outlining athletic muscles. His rib cag
was high and hard, strewn with fine dark hairs that looke
as if they would be wiry to the touch. Not that she intende
to find out.

"Let me help you relax," he offered and rolled her ove
onto her stomach. At least in this position she didn't have
to meet his teasing gaze. But the respite was short-lived

As she buried her face in her folded arms she felt his fingers go to work on the taut muscles of her shoulders and back.

"Some oil would make this easier," he muttered.

Nothing would make this easier, she thought, thankful her hot features were hidden from him. She had moisturizer in her bag, but she wasn't about to volunteer anything. His touch was already sending her senses into overdrive. She tried to relax and focus on her neck muscles, which were slowly unknotting as he worked on them.

It did feel blissful, she had to admit, and that was the problem. A tension headache that had been building, gradually subsided as he kneaded each muscle in turn. But it was at the cost of a much more sensual form of tension which began in the depths of her stomach and spiraled all the way to the top of her head.

When he gave her neck muscles a final squeeze, she felt ready to explode with the need for him to touch her everywhere, not just on the neck and shoulders. "That should help you to sleep."

She could hardly believe it when he rolled back to his side of the bed and snapped off the light. Moments later his even breathing told her he was asleep.

It was what she had wanted, and it was the right thing to do. But it didn't feel right. After the intimacy of his touch she ached with longings she couldn't begin to catalog, and they were as spiritual as they were physical. Being with Nicholas felt right in a way she had never known before.

It didn't help to remind herself that Nicholas was acting honorably and she should respect the iron control which prevented him from giving in to temptation. It wasn't because he lacked passion, she was well aware. Keeping his side of their bargain couldn't have been easy, but he did it, anyway.

Could she do any less for him? The empty feeling inside

her reminded her of the other kind of emptiness in her life, which she couldn't ask him to share. Leaving so he could have the family of his dreams was the right thing to do. She would go as soon as he found a permanent caretaker for Maree.

It came to her that she was sick to death of doing the right thing around Nicholas, when every instinct urged the opposite. But she would do it, anyway. Her desolate sigh whispered into the darkness, and she knew that sleep would elude her for a long time.

Chapter Nine

In the early hours of the morning she slept, awakening to the unfamiliar sensation of an arm resting across her body. The weight was warm and comforting, but it made her far too aware of the hard masculine shape of its owner. During the night they had rolled together and now nestled, spoon fashion, in the hollow in the center of the bed.

For a moment she yearned to be even closer, to have him hold and caress her as a lover, until she remembered the promise she had made to herself last night. This couldn't go on. She was becoming far too involved with Nicholas, when it was the last thing she should do for his sake.

Carefully, to avoid disturbing him, she slid out from beneath his arm and went into the bathroom to shower and dress. Then she left a note on the hotel stationery to say she had gone down to the restaurant for breakfast and would wait for him there. She knew if she stayed in the room any longer, honor was likely to be the first casualty.

He joined her before she had finished her first cup of coffee. His hair gleamed from the shower and even in the clothes he had worn the day before, he looked so attractive that heads turned as he strode across the room to her table. The coffee turned to sawdust in her throat.

"Sleep well?" he asked as he sat down and accepted coffee from a waitress.

Bethany waited until the woman left. "Reasonably well, thank you. And you?"

"I always sleep better with company than I do alone." His eyes danced and he lifted the cup in a mock toast. "Do you realize this is the first time we've slept together?"

She gave him a sharp glance. "We did not sleep together. Well, not in the way you usually use the phrase."

"I don't usually use it, Bethany," he said on a soft note. "At least I haven't for a long time. I guess I was waiting for someone like you to come along and make it attractive again."

Tension riffled through her. "Don't, Nicholas. We can't go on like this."

His fingers tightened around the cup. "Agreed. Last night was hard on both of us." He winced. "Maybe I should put it another way. Last night was hell."

"Yes, it was." But not for the reason he thought. She wasn't asking for a replay of the evening with a different ending, which was what he wanted. "I have to return to Melbourne as soon as you find someone permanent for Maree."

He looked thunderstruck. "Am I going too fast for you? Is it—"

She covered his hand with hers. "It isn't you, it's me. I have—my reasons—for leaving, and last night isn't one of them." If anything, she would treasure the memory for a long, long time.

"There's nothing I can say to change your mind?"

He could say he would be fulfilled with a loving wife and his brother's baby. It was the only thing that could make a difference, and she was glad he didn't say it because it wouldn't be true.

She stood up. "I'm not hungry. I'll get the things from the room and meet you in the lobby after breakfast."

Before she could walk away, a smartly dressed older woman approached them, her expression quizzical. "Nicholas? It is Nicholas Frakes, isn't it?"

He grinned as he got to his feet. "Miss Flynn. It's great to see you again."

The woman made a shushing gesture. "You aren't my high school student any longer. You can call me Georgina." In an aside to Bethany, she added, "He was one of my favorites. Fancy running into you again after all these years."

Nicholas introduced Bethany and invited the older woman to join them for coffee. Bethany reluctantly sat down again but said little as the two caught up on old times. It seemed that Georgina had been living in Melbourne for many years until she was widowed. "I decided to come home to the Central Highlands and look for a live-in position where I can be part of a family as well as earn a living," she concluded.

"Can't you return to teaching?" Nicholas asked.

Georgina Flynn shook her head. "At my age, I don't need the pressure. A family with a small baby is my idea of Heaven nowadays."

"Then maybe I can help." Bethany could practically hear Nicholas's thoughts and her heart almost stopped. Somehow she knew Georgina would make the perfect nanny for Maree. In growing despair, she heard Nicholas sketch in Maree's background and explain what he needed.

Bethany knew she should be happy to have convinced him that she didn't want the job, but when Georgina accepted it, Bethany wanted to weep. It meant she had no further reason to remain at Yarrawong. Acting as if the decision pleased her was almost more than she could manage.

"You don't have to leave. You can stay as long as you like, finish your article on the dollhouse," he offered when she accounted her intention to move on.

"It's finished," she said flatly, knowing she meant more than the article. "Now you have Georgina, there's nothing to keep me here."

His heated gaze flayed her. "Nothing?"

She lifted her head. "You've been wonderful, Nicholas. The right to publish the plans to the Frakes Baby House will make all the difference to me."

He looked as if it cost him a lot to say, "Then all I can do is wish you well."

"You're stark, staring mad," her brother Sam railed when she called at his factory to collect her mail and inform him that she had officially left Yarrawong. "From what you tell me, Nicholas Frakes didn't want you to leave. In fact, it sounded as if he wanted something a lot more permanent from you."

"What he wants is a family, the one thing I can't provide. Can we change the subject?" she implored. She hitched herself onto one of Sam's hand-carved bar stools and leafed through the letters that had accumulated since Sam forwarded the last batch to Yarrawong. "Bills, bills, more bills. Couldn't you save me more exciting mail than this, Sam?"

He pulled a letter out of his pocket and held it aloft. "This might cheer you up. It's from the Hollander Publishing Group."

She reached for it, but he held it away. "What's it about? You obviously already know."

He grinned. "You told me to open anything that looked

important.'' He took out a single sheet of expensive-looking letterhead. ''It says, 'Dear Ms. Dale...'''

Impatience got the better of her and she snatched it from his hands, scanning the letter with growing amazement. ''Hollander Publishing want to make an offer for the journal and turn it into a big-circulation magazine with me as a consulting editor. They've asked for a meeting on the...good grief it's today's date. I'm supposed to be there this afternoon.''

''I tried to call you but you had already left Yarrawong, and I didn't know where to get in touch with you.''

''I called in at the folks' place on the way back and ended up staying overnight. You know our family. There's no such thing as a flying visit by the time everybody's caught up on everybody else's news. What shall I do about this meeting?''

''Attend it,'' Sam suggested dryly. ''Hollander must think your journal has a big future or they wouldn't be after it, and you.''

Nicholas's parting prediction echoed through her mind— watch out Rupert Murdoch. It had been truer than he knew. A month earlier this news would have filled her with excitement. Now it felt anticlimactic. Although she had told Nicholas it was her dream, she wasn't sure if it was what she wanted anymore. Thanks to him she had never felt more confused in her life.

''I'd better go home and change,'' she said, because Sam seemed to expect some sort of reaction. ''This definitely calls for power dressing.''

Her brother rested a hand on her arm. ''Forget the power dressing, little sister, and just be yourself. Remember, just because Hollander Publications wants to buy your journal doesn't mean you have to sell it to them.''

She stared at him uncomfortably. ''How do you know what I'm thinking?''

"Let's say I've known you a long time. You look like you're about to lose something, instead of gaining your heart's desire."

She had already lost more than he could ever know. "It was my heart's desire once, and I still want the journal to succeed, but…"

"But not if the price is your freedom." His glance encompassed the small factory and the handful of craftspeople who worked for him, not for high wages, but for the love of producing work of which they could be proud. "Why do you think I persevere with Dale Designs in spite of all the work and worry?"

"Because you love making beautiful furniture."

"I love the pleasure people take in my furniture," he amended. "This isn't about working in wood any more than your journal is about dollhouses. It's about sharing a passion and improving people's lives just a little. Making a difference is what it's really about."

She felt shaken. "That's the longest speech I've ever heard you give, big brother."

"As long as you can remember it when the corporate world dangles its carrots in front of your nose." He gave her a playful shove. "Now get out of here. I have work to do." His face became flushed. "Before you go I have one other bit of news. I'm getting married."

Her mouth dropped open. "You're what? Sam, that's fantastic. Who is she?"

"Remember Amanda? She's mad as a wet hen, doesn't do any more work than she must, and I love her madly."

Bethany flung her arms around her brother. "When? You know the family will want a huge wedding with all the frills."

He frowned. "They'll have to live without it. I'm not turning this into a three-ring circus. Amanda's pregnant so we want a simple ceremony as soon as we can arrange it."

She only heard one thing. "You're going to be a daddy?"

His grin broadened. "Sure am. It was an accident, but I couldn't be happier. The ultrasound tests show we're having a boy. A son."

"Is Amanda pleased?"

"She was worried until I assured her I want the baby—and her—more than anything in the world. Now she's as happy as I am." His eyes danced. "Pity we can't make it a double wedding with you and Nicholas."

They couldn't because there would be no babies for them. Sam's joy at his news only emphasized the rightness of her decision. If she allowed herself to become involved with Nicholas he would never know the joy she saw on Sam's face now at knowing his baby was on the way. She l...liked Nicholas too much to do that to him.

Then it hit her with the force of a truck slamming into a brick wall. She didn't *like* Nicholas. She *loved* him. Nothing else could explain the intensity of her feelings. Everything else paled into insignificance beside it. Not even the offer from Hollander Publishing could lift her to the same dizzy heights as spending one night in his arms at a hotel.

She would trade every bit of commercial success for the right to spend every night with him, she was finally forced to admit. Why hadn't she seen it before? Nothing less than love could give her the strength to walk away and leave him free to have the family of his dreams.

Sam regarded her worriedly. "What is it, little sister? You look as if you've seen a ghost."

Perhaps she had—the ghost of her hopes and dreams. Now she understood her driving need to get away from Yarrawong, before she gave herself away and admitted that leaving was the last thing she wanted to do. Loving Nicholas as she did, there was nothing else she could do and live with herself afterward.

"I'm fine," she assured her brother huskily, sliding off the stool. "It's time I got ready for this meeting. Wish me luck."

He hugged her. "Good luck—if it's what you want."

"Of course it's what I want. Don't forget to send me an invitation to the wedding."

"And the christening. You will be godmother, of course?"

A pain settled in the area around her heart but she nodded. "I'll be the best godmother any baby ever had," she promised.

The thought stayed with her as she prepared for the meeting that afternoon with the publisher. Until now the journal had been her baby, more a labor of love rather than a business, a bit like Sam's furniture factory. Did she really want to see it turned into a mass-circulation glossy magazine with a power-dressed version of herself at the helm?

It was the story she'd told Nicholas, but was it the future she really wanted? She couldn't have children, but it didn't mean she couldn't have a family at all. Until Alexander reacted so badly she had intended to foster or adopt children, as her own parents had done. They had believed it was unfair to keep having more children, when there were already so many children needing love and care.

Not all men were like her parents, willing to accept another's child as their own, although having three natural children first may have made it easier. She wished it wasn't so hard to talk to her father about personal matters so they could have discussed how men felt about such things. Despite coming to Australia as a child and marrying an Australian woman, he still had the Welsh habit of keeping his innermost thoughts to himself.

Nicholas had taken Maree into his heart without a second thought, but then she was his brother's child, and he expected to have his own children, as well. Knowing how much she loved him, Bethany couldn't deny him that right, whatever the cost to herself.

She was glad to have the publisher's meeting to prepare for, because it took her mind off Nicholas. He would haunt her dreams for many nights to come, but for now, she could focus on the business at hand. One day at a time, she told herself. It was the only way she could see herself getting through the lonely times ahead.

Angus Hollander, the son of the founder of Hollander Publishing, showed her into his office on the top floor of a Southgate office tower that boasted a spectacular view across the Yarra River.

He heard her sharp intake of breath. "If our discussions go well today, you could have an office like this, and sooner than you probably expect," he informed her.

"It's impressive," she said, but couldn't see herself in such a sterile setting. She took a seat across the desk from him. Sam might not approve of power dressing, but her navy suit and cerise shirt was absolutely right for this high-powered atmosphere.

She leafed through the offer document placed in front of her but without much enthusiasm. Angus Hollander would be surprised to know she had come with every intention of turning the offer down. Sam was right. *The Baby House* was more craft than business. It might never become her fortune but neither would she have to drag herself to work each day to earn a paycheck from someone else.

She leaned forward. "Before we begin, Mr. Hollander, I'd like to know how you became aware of my journal. The circulation is still relatively modest."

He smiled. "I'm glad you said 'still.' We're planning to boost it considerably once you come on board. Let's say I heard about you from a friend with whom I serve on a state government instrumentality."

Alarm bells sounded in her head. "The friend wouldn't be Nicholas Frakes, by any chance?"

The publisher looked surprised. "As a matter of fact it would. He asked me not to mention his involvement because he said you'd insist on your work being judged on its own merit. Which, of course, it is, or we wouldn't be having this meeting." He flicked through a file on his desk that she saw held recent copies of her journal. "Nicholas did me a favor, bringing your work to my notice. You have a wonderful eye for layout and design. Do you handle all the feature writing, as well?"

"I have little choice. *The Baby House* is produced with a staff of one," she pointed out. "Not having a lot of capital, I can't give up my day job yet," she added with wry humor. Only this morning she had called Stella Trioli at the children's shelter to find out whether her casual job was still open. Stella had wryly told her that no one else was willing to work for the meager salary the center's budget allowed, so Bethany could return as soon as she was ready, working the same hours as before.

Angus Hollander's smile widened. "If your journal becomes a Hollander publication you can count on giving up your day job. And quite possibly your evenings and weekends as well. Nine-to-five people don't last long here. You need to live and breathe publishing." He paused, regarding her over rimless glasses. "Nicholas gives me the impression you'd fit right in."

Her heart sank. Nicholas had bought the fiction of her career-mindedness, hook, line and sinker. Or had he? A new suspicion was dawning. What if he had arranged this meeting to test whether or not she had told him the truth?

She was caught between a rock and a hard place. Or a hard man. If she accepted Hollander's offer she as good as sold her soul to the devil. If she turned them down, Nicholas would know she wasn't as ambitious as she claimed.

But why go to so much trouble? Why couldn't he simply accept that they weren't right for each other and let her go off into the night? Was this some kind of macho thing, to satisfy himself that she was the problem and not him? As quickly as she hatched the thought, she dismissed it. Nicholas was one of the most secure people she'd ever met. If he agreed with her opinion of him, well and good. If he didn't, she was welcome to it, anyway. It wouldn't change his self-image one iota.

Unless he loved her, too. The thought made her throat spasm, and she choked, prompting Angus Hollander to offer her a glass of water. She nodded her thanks and sipped it slowly, needing time to think. If Nicholas had fallen in love with her, it was all the more important to keep her distance. Loving her had a price she wasn't prepared to let him pay.

"Your offer is an interesting one," she said when she could speak normally again. "I'll want my business adviser to look it over before I give you an answer." Sam would love being elevated to business adviser.

Angus Hollander nodded as if it was no more than he would have done. "Just as long as your answer is the right one." He stood up. "Magazine publishing is getting more and more specialized. Niche publications like yours have a big future that's still largely unexploited. If you don't bring your dollhouse journal under our umbrella we may have to start one of our own."

It was said with a smile, but she heard the underlying threat. She could join them, but she couldn't beat them. She was sure Nicholas hadn't foreseen this outcome when he recommended her to Hollander Publishing. She had only herself to blame for making him think it was what she wanted. But she had never dreamed the price would be so high.

Chapter Ten

"Come on little darling, eat your spinach. You love spinach. Here, you can even have it with banana."

Nicholas watched in growing exasperation as Maree upended the bowl onto the floor. Not even allowing her to feed herself had made a difference this morning. Not for the first time, he wondered what secret women knew to achieve these miracles that men hadn't yet discovered. Georgina, his old schoolteacher and now Maree's nanny, didn't seem to have this much trouble getting her charge to eat. Unfortunately, Georgina was at the dentist this morning, so he was on his own.

He picked up the bowl and exchanged it for a clean one, noting that the kitchen wasn't as pristine as he had gotten used to since Kylie took over the housekeeping. She wasn't due in until this afternoon, either, although he couldn't remember why he'd given her the morning off. He expelled a heavy breath. Had he become so helpless that he couldn't manage without these women in his life?

It wasn't women, it was woman, he told himself grimly.

He could do without almost anyone, except the one woman who had walked out of his life for good. "You miss Bethany, too, don't you, little darling?" he asked Maree.

Was it his imagination or did she perk up at once? "Beh, beh, beh, beh," she chanted. The new sound seemed to please her so she repeated it, "Beh, beh, beh, beh."

"Are you trying to say Bethany? Me, too," he agreed glumly. "It won't help either of us. She isn't coming back. We couldn't compete with a dollhouse magazine, of all things." In sheer frustration he threw a balled up tea towel at the wall. "Who'd ever believe I could be bested by a dollhouse magazine?"

Maree watched the tea towel slide down the wall. "Beh, beh, beh, beh."

He spooned more food into the clean bowl. "Maybe you'll eat this for Bethany."

Maree looked at it with interest, then fisted the spoon and dug into the green porridge. "Beh, beh, beh, beh." For one moment he thought the magic name had induced her to cooperate until she threw the whole lot at the wall where the tea towel had landed.

He let his jaw drop as he stared at the mess, then began to laugh. "Like father, like daughter, eh, Maree?"

She didn't care whether Daddy was laughing in humor or hysteria. Maree was happy to join in, and the sight of her pleasure lifted his spirits slightly. It wasn't a lot, because they had a long way to lift before they hit depressed, even. But he felt a little better afterward.

He was starting on baby breakfast number three when the telephone rang. He reached for it and tucked the receiver into the angle between his shoulder and chin. "Nicholas Frakes."

There was a pause. "I was given this number for Bethany Dale. Is she available?"

The woman's tone was briskly professional, and Nicholas's senses went on instant alert. "Who is this?"

"It's the Southgate Fertility Clinic. To whom am I speaking?"

He didn't stop to think. "I'm Dr. Nicholas Frakes, Bethany's fiancé. She isn't here at present. She's—at the dentist." He glanced at Maree who gave every sign of rapt attention to the conversation. Lying was one skill he hoped she wouldn't copy from him. It wasn't something he normally practiced but the word *clinic* mentioned in connection with Bethany had chilled him to the core. He needed to know why she was getting a call from a medical facility.

"Will you ask her to call Dr. Jamison about her test results?"

He felt as if someone had kicked him in the stomach. "Test results? Look, we're heading off overseas as soon as she gets back. You'd better give me the results and I'll make sure she gets them."

There was another pause. "Under the circumstances, and you, being her fiancé, I suppose it's all right, Dr. Frakes. It might be better if she does hear it from you, rather than an impartial source. She's bound to need support."

"She'll have all the support I can give her," he vowed, meaning it with all his heart. His mind was racing. Was Bethany ill? Was it the real reason she had been so anxious to get away?

"Then please tell her that all the results are negative. Without surgery she has no chance of conceiving a child naturally, and only a one-in-three chance with the operation, so frankly, her doctor can't recommend the risk for someone who is otherwise perfectly healthy. There are other avenues to explore, but she can discuss them when you return from your trip."

Trip? His thoughts were so overloaded that he almost

betrayed himself. "Of course, the trip. I'll give Bethany your message."

"Thank you, Dr. Frakes."

"You're welcome."

She wasn't welcome at all, he thought as he hung up the phone. For most women this would be devastating news, although he was having trouble thinking past the "perfectly healthy" part. For a moment he'd thought...

He sat down as his legs weakened. Bethany was perfectly healthy. Hang on to that. She wasn't dying. She was only infertile. Then it hit him. The woman he loved—he may as well face it, there was no other explanation for the whirl-wind of feelings tearing through him—the woman he loved couldn't have babies. He stared at Maree in astonishment. "Now I know why Bethany left, and it's my fault," he told the baby.

She tilted her head to one side, "Beh, beh, beh?"

"Yes, Bethany. She left because of my big mouth." How many times had he talked to her about wanting children? Every time he mentioned it must have been like a blow to her.

He hadn't meant to hurt her, but did it make any differ-ence? He knew which road was paved with good intentions because he was on it right now. How could he have been so blind? He did want children, lots of them. But more than anything in the world he wanted Bethany. He would rather have her and no babies than a cast the size of *The Sound of Music* and no Bethany in his life.

Restlessness surged through him. It was all he could do not to pace. Georgina wouldn't be back for another hour, but as soon as she returned to look after Maree he would head for Melbourne. He had promised to deliver the test results to Bethany, and he always kept his promises.

"It's chaos around here today," Stella complained as she skirted a ladder and buckets of paint cluttering the hall of the Williamstown Infants' Shelter. The historic building was badly run down and Stella had decided that they could no longer postpone the most urgent repairs and redecorating.

Bethany gave her boss a wan smile. "I picked the right time to come back to work."

"I'm grateful you did. I've been running things practically single-handedly and can't hope to attract anyone permanent until the decorating is finished. I'm glad you agreed to fill in because I really needed the help in the meantime. Are you sure I can't persuade you to come back to stay, even part-time?"

Bethany shook her head. "It's crunch time for me. I have to decide what to do with the rest of my life."

Stella's eyebrows arched. "Sounds serious. I take it child care is not on the list."

"I love working with the kids here but..."

"It isn't everybody's idea of a life's work," Stella supplied. "Don't worry, I won't pressure you to stay more than once a day, until we get back to a full complement of babies, then I may step it up to once an hour."

"Thanks for the warning," Bethany said wryly. Stella had placed as many of the children as possible in temporary foster care while the shelter was given its long-overdue facelift. Even so, five children under the age of two remained, so Bethany didn't blame Stella for trying to persuade her to stay. The wages were low and conditions demanding and funds were always at crisis level, so Stella was accustomed to using every trick in the book to keep things running. Where the children were concerned she had no pride and few scruples.

They flattened themselves against a wall as a workman came past carrying another ladder. Stella's voice stopped him in midstride. "Just a minute, young man."

He turned. "Sorry about the disruption but you know what they say about omelettes and eggs?"

"I know what they say about smoking around young children," Stella snapped back. With a look of distaste, she plucked the cigarette out of the man's mouth, dropped it and ground it underfoot. "The first things I want put back on the walls are the No Smoking signs."

The painter glanced at the mangled remains of his cigarette and seemed about to argue until he saw Stella's face. "Whatever you say, lady."

"*Dr.* Trioli," she shot back. "How much longer is this going to take?"

The painter practically stood at attention, his ladder held like a shouldered weapon. "Another day and a half at most. If I could bring in more people..."

"A day and a half is fine," Stella conceded. Bethany knew the budget didn't stretch to employing more tradespeople. "But no more smoking indoors, understood?"

"Sure lady...er, Doctor," he amended.

"And could you take a look at my office door? It's sticking badly. It took me ten minutes to get it open this morning."

The man looked relieved at being offered a way to redeem himself. "I can't do it today if you want the painting finished, but I'll fix it first thing tomorrow." He took his ladder and himself off before Stella could think of anything else for him to do.

Bethany stifled a laugh. "You're a tough lady... Doctor." But there was admiration in her tone. It must be wonderful to have the courage of your convictions like Stella, able to steer a straight course through life, certain of your purpose, Bethany thought. Stella was a lot like Sam, she recognized belatedly. Both were people of vision. Neither of them cared about money, fame or what people thought.

Suddenly she knew what she was going to tell Angus Hollander. He could take his offer and...produce his own magazine if he wanted to. She would simply make hers better to ride out the competition, she resolved. It wouldn't be easy, but it would be more satisfying than selling out her vision.

She smiled at her boss, feeling light of heart for the first time since leaving Nicholas. "Thanks, Stella."

The older woman looked mystified. "Whatever it was I said...you're welcome."

The rest of the day passed in a whirl of activity as Bethany tried to entertain the babies while keeping them clean, fed and out of the way of the tradespeople. She had put the last of the children to bed in an improvised dormitory, since the regular bedrooms were off-limits for the time being. She was shaking plaster dust out of her hair when Stella stuck her head around the door. "I'll take over here until the night nurse arrives. You have a visitor, Bethany."

"It had better be Sam," she muttered. At least he would understand why she looked as if she needed shelter rather than working in one. The parts of her that weren't gritty with renovation debris were splattered with baby food. Fortunately, her apron had suffered the worst of the damage so she removed it and hung it behind a door, then raked her fingers through her hair in a futile attempt to tidy it.

Her heart almost stopped as she recognized the tall, masculine figure prowling around the entrance hall, dodging painters' equipment. "Nicholas, what are you doing here?"

The corners of his mouth tilted upward as he took in her bedraggled appearance. "I'm fine, thanks. It's good to see you, too. You look wonderful."

She tried to resist, but his presence lifted her spirits to dizzying heights. She felt instantly more alive and more aware of her appearance. Until he arrived, it hadn't troubled her nearly as much. "I doubt it. I look like something the cat dragged in."

His eyes never left her face. She wondered fleetingly if he even noticed the rest of her appearance. "The cat can drag you into my place anytime."

Cotton wool filled her throat. "What do you want?" Then another thought seized her. "Is Maree all right?"

"She's fine. I left her in Georgina's capable hands while I came to see you. I'm taking you out to dinner."

Cinderella's finery wouldn't have prepared her to go to dinner with him. She had barely started coming to terms with a future without him in it. A dinner date would undo the slight progress she'd managed to make. She took refuge in her looks. "I can't go out looking like this."

"You look fine. Your boss told me you should have gone home half an hour ago, so get your things and let's go."

"Go where? Why?"

He finally noticed that paint flakes weren't a normal part of her outfit, but he took it in his stride. "We'll go somewhere where you don't have to dress up. We need to talk."

Knowing how much she loved him, talk was way down the list of things she wanted from him but it was far and away the safest. Since he wasn't taking no for an answer, she fetched her handbag and disappeared into the ladies' room to tidy up as best she could.

He had retreated to the street by the time she emerged, and she couldn't help feeling a warm glow at the appreciation in his gaze as she came down the steps. Most of the paint flakes had shaken off her practical navy skirt and buttermilk lace blouse, and a quick brush had restored some of the gloss to her tangled curls. A quick dash of long-wearing lipstick, the kind which didn't come off when you were kissed, she noted wryly, and she was ready, outwardly at least. Inwardly was another matter. She felt as if two opposing armies had set up camp in her stomach and were preparing to do battle.

In contrast, Nicholas looked infuriatingly confident and in control. He smiled, and her heart turned over. "Ready?"

"Depends what for."

"Dinner, talk, exactly what I promised you."

She shook off a sense of disappointment. Whatever had brought him here wasn't going to change their situation. Better to think of this evening as a gift, another memory to store away against the lonely times ahead.

Williamstown was a sleepy seaport, once destined to be the heart of Melbourne, but now a tourist haunt at the mouth of the Yarra River across the majestic West Gate Bridge. With its iron-lace-clad houses, tree-lined streets, wharfs and piers, it still looked the way the rest of Melbourne had looked a hundred years ago.

The shelter was located a short way from the tourist streets of Nelson Place and the Strand, and Nicholas led her toward them. Along the waterfront promenade were any number of restaurants, coffee shops and pubs where dress rules tended to stop at shoes and a shirt. She began to worry less about how she was dressed and more about what she could possibly say to Nicholas without giving herself away.

Knowing she loved him made it harder than ever to keep up the fiction of being too ambitious to settle down. She only hoped he had some other problem on his mind.

He took her to a café called Settlers. Inside, it had a warm, old-fashioned feel with lace curtains, an open log fire for the winter, and memorabilia from the 1850s adorning the walls. She followed Nicholas through the main room to a leafy courtyard opening off one side with private tables overlooking the sea.

When they had dealt with the menu, she gave him a troubled look. "What's this all about?"

"First, tell me how you got on with Angus Hollander," he prompted.

She was glad to be served their first course of lobsters on a butter-lettuce salad before framing her answer. "His offer is generous, but I need to think it over."

He toyed with the salad. "I thought you'd jump at the chance to move into the big time with your magazine. It is what you want, isn't it?"

What was he getting at? "Of course it is." She hoped she sounded more certain to him than to herself. "It was kind of you to recommend my work."

"Not kind, practical. It's called networking. You'll get the hang of it once you start working with Hollander. He believes in lobbying in a big way. It isn't altruism that keeps him serving on those government committees."

"So I gathered. He as good as warned me if I don't give him *The Baby House,* he'll start one of his own."

She hadn't intended to tell him about the threat. With Nicholas, it was alarmingly easy to let her guard down. If she wasn't careful she would end up telling him far more than she should.

Anger simmered in his dark gaze. "I know he's a tough negotiator, but that's pretty low."

She affected a shrug. "My subscribers want specialist information, not glossy pictures. Any magazine he starts may outsell me, but I'm determined to survive."

"You sound as if the decision's already made. What happened to your plans to conquer the publishing world?"

She reached for a glass of water. "Angus Hollander's way isn't the only way to succeed in this business."

He held her gaze for a long moment. "It's the fast lane to the top, which you're supposed to want more than anything else."

Panic ate at her, and it was all she could do to remain seated. "Supposed? You sound as if you doubt it."

His fingers tightened around his water glass until she thought the stem would shatter. ''I've always doubted it, and this time I'm not giving up until I get the truth.''

She played with the seafood dish that had been set in front of her, her appetite gone. She couldn't tell him the truth. Either he would reject her outright or he would say it didn't matter, that they could still have a future. No matter how much she wanted to hear it, she loved him too deeply to let him give up so much on her account.

''I'm waiting, Bethany.''

''Nicholas, I...''

Whatever she would have said was drowned out by the banshee wail of sirens coming closer and closer. A fire engine tore past the restaurant, lights and sirens blazing. They stopped abruptly a short distance away. Around them diners spilled out onto the street to see what was happening. One of them came back to the next table. ''Looks like the children's shelter is on fire,'' he told his companion.

Bethany felt the color leave her face. Nicholas didn't hesitate. He tossed a handful of banknotes onto the table and grabbed her hand. ''Come on. They could need our help.''

Her own cares were forgotten as she clung to his hand, following in the path his determined progress cleared for them. She only prayed they would be in time.

Chapter Eleven

By the time they rounded the corner, the fire was a living creature, feeding on the old building that housed the children's shelter. Its hot breath fanned them as they reached the end of the cobbled laneway, the narrow access hampering the firefighters' attempts to move their equipment closer to the fire.

"The whole back of the building is on fire. The children!" Bethany gasped. She grabbed the nearest firefighter, pulled out her identification and thrust it forward. "I work here."

"How many people were inside?" the firefighter asked.

"Five children, two adults." The painters had left before Bethany, leaving only Stella and the night nurse.

The firefighter relayed the details to her colleagues and allowed Bethany and Nicholas to approach a little closer. "The boss tells me the night nurse already got the kids out. They were in a front room, and the fire started at the back so they're unharmed, but the paramedics are checking them over to be on the safe side."

"What about Stella?"

"Who's Stella?"

"Dr. Stella Trioli, the center's director," Nicholas supplied. He looked over the shoulder of the firefighter to the flames consuming the rear of the century-old building then ducked, pulling Bethany down with him and covering her with his body as something exploded inside. "The paint cans must be feeding it." Bethany nodded.

"We'll get this woman if she's still in there," she was told. "The best thing you can do is stay out of harm's way."

Minutes passed with no sign of the older woman. Crouched behind a sheltering wall, Bethany traded desperate glances with Nicholas. "What if Stella's trapped inside somewhere?" She was horrified at how reedy her voice sounded over the fire's roar.

He looked grim. "Could she have gone home?"

"Stella never goes home on time. She lives...lives and breathes for these children."

Nicholas stood up, and fear shafted through Bethany. "You can't mean to go in there? You heard the firefighter."

"Where's the most likely place to find Stella?"

"Her office is the window closest to the rear on this side, but—"

"Wait here."

"Nicholas, no." Either he didn't hear her over the locomotive roar of the fire or he wasn't listening. He kept going.

Radiant heat from the road seeped through the soles of her shoes, but she registered only his commanding figure striding unhesitatingly toward the building. She stood up to watch his lithe movements, and waves of heat poured over her. Her smoke-seared throat closed. He was here because of her, risking his life in a place he should never have been.

If anything happened to him she would never forgive herself.

There was only one thing to do. Covering her nose and mouth with a handkerchief, she followed him. She knew the layout of the shelter better than anyone. There must be some way she could help.

The firefighters were busy with the back section and no one tried to stop her. Inside, the smoke was blinding. She made her way more by touch than sight, almost falling over painting debris in the halls. When she reached it, Stella's office door refused to open. "Nicholas?" she called over the roar of the fire.

"In here. Door slammed shut behind me," he called back. "Stella's alive but unconscious, probably from the smoke."

Bethany fought the door but the century-old timber resisted. Even before Stella complained about it sticking this morning, it had always been difficult. Now it was impossible. "It's no use, it won't budge," she called.

"Try the window. I'll meet you there."

She raced back outside and around to Stella's office window. Nicholas was already there, Stella in his arms. Bethany looked around frantically, then picked up a loose brick. She held it up so he would see what she intended to do. He turned his back, sheltering Stella from the glass as Bethany shattered the window and cleared as much broken glass as she could from the frame with the brick.

Moments later he passed the unconscious woman to her and clambered out himself, then took Stella from her. "We've got to get to the ambulance."

"This way."

The paramedics met them halfway and transferred Stella to a stretcher. Coming to consciousness, she coughed and fought them, and Bethany felt fresh tears sting her eyes. "You saved her life."

Nicholas ignored the compliment. "Are you all right?"

"You're asking me? You walk into a burning building that's falling down around you and you ask *me* if I'm okay? You could have been killed." She couldn't stop her voice from cracking.

He heard it and took her arms. "It's all right, Bethany. I'm all right."

His strong grip was so welcome, she couldn't doubt it. "Yes, you are, thank goodness. For a while, I thought…"

"Then don't think. You took a big risk yourself. I thought I told you to stay put." His gentle, admiring tone belied the chiding words. He looked at the babies gathered around the night nurse in the shelter of the ambulance. "What are these children going to do? The building looks like it won't be habitable for some time."

"It was bad enough before. The fire must have started among the paint things," she said, remembering a painter's cigarette this morning. If he had lit another one in defiance of Stella's orders, then dropped it somewhere… She dismissed the speculation. The experts would establish what happened, and the center was insured. Nicholas was right, the children were their most pressing concern.

She chewed her lower lip. "We used up all our emergency accommodation relocating the children before the renovations started. These five are here because they have nowhere else to go."

"Then there's only one place to take them—home with me."

"To Yarrawong?" She remembered the rooms that had been intended as tourist accommodations. "Are you sure?"

He nodded and turned to Stella who was recovering rapidly and resisting the paramedic's attempts to convince her to go to the hospital for observation. "We'll need your authority to take the children to my property, Dr. Trioli."

She gave it readily, gesturing weakly from the stretcher.

"Luckily the shelter's minibus was parked around the corner, out of the fire's path." She fumbled in her pocket and proffered a car key. "Take it, it should hold everyone."

The paramedic finally convinced her to accept treatment. She gave Nicholas a wry look. "Medical people always want to meddle. I'll come and see you as soon as they let me." Coughing, she grasped his hand. "Thank you for saving me. It was foolhardy but I'm not going to complain."

He returned the doctor's weak clasp. "You concentrate on recovering. The children will be fine with Bethany and me until you can make proper arrangements."

Stella's gaze went from Nicholas to Bethany. "Seeing you together, I understand why she won't rejoin my staff. Can't say I blame her." She started to cough again, and the paramedics insisted on loading her into the ambulance without any more delays.

After they left, Nicholas fetched the minibus and they put the children aboard. Bethany stared transfixed at the smoldering ruins being guarded by the firefighters. Nicholas took her arm. "Come on. You can't do any more here."

He was right, and she let him help her aboard the bus. It was equipped with a car phone, which he used to alert Georgina to expect them. Kylie had left for the day, but the night nurse from the shelter agreed to follow them in her own car.

A few hours ago she had thought she would never see Nicholas again, far less be driving back to Yarrawong with him. It was almost too much to take in. Belatedly it dawned on her that she had nothing with her other than the clothes she was wearing.

With the babies strapped into an assortment of safety seats in the roomy bus, a detour was unthinkable, so there was nothing to be done about it. This was the second unplanned night she would spend with him, she realized. It was also likely to be the last night of any kind they would have together.

Georgina met them at the door and helped to carry the children to the rooms she had prepared since receiving Nicholas's phone call. The children were hungry and, even with four pairs of hands, it was some time before they were all fed, changed and settled again for what remained of the night.

Watching Nicholas tend to the last infant, Bethany felt a tug around the region of her heart. He held the small boy against his shoulder, looking so attractive and natural that desire slammed through her. She loved Nicholas, wanting him and the babies he dreamed of having, more than she had ever wanted anything.

Ramming her knuckles against her mouth to stifle the sounds welling in her throat, she shouldered her way out of the room.

By a superhuman effort of will, she got her runaway emotions under control by the time Nicholas joined her on the veranda. She was glad of the shadows hiding the expression in her eyes from his searching inspection. He stretched and leaned against the waist-high railing. "What a night."

"Everyone asleep?" Her voice sounded hollow.

He nodded tiredly. "They seem to do everything in series. Wake up, eat, sleep."

She nodded. "It's the same at the shelter. If one starts to cry, soon they all join in."

He turned his head. "What did Stella mean when she said she couldn't persuade you to rejoin the staff?"

Her heart pounded loudly enough to muffle the night sounds coming from the surrounding bushland. "I'm thinking over my options. I still haven't decided what to do about Angus Hollander's offer."

"Yes, you have," he said quietly, reaching to draw her close to him.

The instant he touched her, her senses ran riot. Although her breathing became fast and shallow, she willed her muscles to relax. Stiffening at his touch was far too betraying. "You seem to know more about my plans than I do."

"I know you aren't going to work for Angus," he said bluntly.

Keeping herself from tensing made her muscles ache. "I'm not?"

"You don't have the killer instinct for it. And besides, you're going to stay here with me."

What was he getting at? "Naturally, I'll help with the babies until Stella finds alternative places for them all." She longed to collapse against him and agree to stay forever if he wanted, but after seeing him with the children tonight she knew she couldn't ask it of him. Deliberately she moved out of the warm circle of his embrace. "Can we talk about this in the morning? I mean, later?" It was already morning. The first fingers of dawn were already staining the sky with gold. "Right now I can't think beyond a shower and a long rest."

He straightened and caught her hand. "I have a better idea. Come with me."

His fingers closing around hers triggered a mixture of alarm and excitement. She had no idea what he had in mind, and it was risky to go anywhere with him, feeling the way she did. The safest place she could possibly go was to bed—alone.

"We're both exhausted," she tried, "can't it wait until later?"

"No, it can't." He sounded boyishly enthusiastic as he towed her off the veranda and down to his four-wheel-drive. It was unlocked, and he helped her into the passenger seat. She regarded him with increasing concern. "Where are we going?'' They were both grimy and soot streaked from the fire. She even had cinders in her hair.

He ignored her protests and started the car. ''You'll find out. Hang on, the road gets rough from here.''

It couldn't get much rougher than the one she was on with him, she reflected as he steered the vehicle along a narrow track through paddocks toward a thick stand of eucalypt forest. Every time they hit a bump in the road she was thrown against him, the contact sending electric arcs of awareness through her body.

Warmth flooded through her in spite of the predawn coolness. She tried to pull in deep breaths, tell herself she could do this, admire whatever view he wanted to show her, without giving her true feelings away.

It didn't help that every time their bodies collided she endured a wave of sensual longing so powerful that she had to clench her hands together to stop them from shaking. ''Have we far to go?'' she asked, hoping he would blame the tremor in her voice on the jarring of the Jeep on the corrugated track.

''Almost there.'' He made it sound like a message, although, for the life of her, she couldn't decipher what it was.

She distracted herself by focusing on the ghostly outlines of gum trees, acacias and tea trees. Graceful wallabies bounded between the trees, which were alive with birds at this hour—pink-streaked galahs, flame robins and chattering finches. In spite of her exhaustion, it felt oddly exhilarating to be awake and about at dawn, and she knew that part of the feeling came from the man at her side.

The track dipped toward a river and emerged into a clearing where a perfect pool steamed in the early-morning light, the rising sun burnishing the surface with gold. Their arrival disturbed the finches and native birds drinking at the water's edge, and they lifted in clouds overhead. She caught her breath and turned moist eyes to Nicholas. "I've never seen anything so beautiful." He couldn't know it, but she recognized the pool as a fittingly glorious place in which to end their association.

He stopped the car and they walked to the water's edge. "It's warm," she discovered, dipping her hand into the shallows. "The pool must be fed from an underground hot spring."

He nodded, his silken look sliding over her. "Better than a shower."

Panic roiled through her. "I can't swim here. I didn't bring a suit." Given the way she felt about him, anything else didn't bear thinking about.

He dismissed the argument. "I can't speak for yours but the women's underwear I've seen in shop windows lately is more modest than most swimwear. But as you wish. I'm going in."

With economical movements he stripped off his soot-streaked trousers and shirt. She averted her eyes as his hands went to the black briefs underneath, but he was only hitching them up. Although it was hardly progress, the action emphasized his overwhelming masculinity.

She felt giddy with the urge to run her hands over his sculpted chest and draw him close to feel his hardness melding with her softness. The misty glade was a Garden of Eden, and she felt as wanton as Eve with the apple in her hand.

Maybe a swim was a good idea after all. She took refuge behind a stunted acacia bush to shed her skirt and blouse, which were as grimy as his clothes. Her coffee-colored bra and panties were more decent than some bikinis, but she still felt exposed as she padded along the bank to a crescent of beach leading into the water. It didn't help to have him watching every movement, and she was glad when the water closed around her.

He stroked lazily over to her, turning onto his back to float. "Told you it feels good. Reviving and relaxing all at once."

The water felt good, but she was anything but relaxed as she swam lengths of slow breaststroke. She wished she dared try floating in the tepid water, but she felt more protected with the water safely up to her neck. The night's events were swiftly catching up, and she was tired to the bone, not least because everything she was giving up was right beside her. If she stretched out her hand...

She headed for the shore. "I'm clean enough. If I stay in here much longer the heat will put me to sleep." Or wake up feelings that were better left dormant for good.

Water streamed off his muscular form as he followed her back to the car. There he produced towels, which she used to soak up most of the moisture before wrapping hers sarong-style around herself. She shivered, but more with reaction to him than with cold.

He draped his towel around her shoulders and began to rub, sending fresh coils of sensual heat through her until she wanted to beg him to stop—or to keep going and never to stop. Neither made much sense anymore.

He knotted a towel around his waist and rummaged in the car. "I brought breakfast, too."

"You thought of everything."

He regarded her dryly. "Almost everything. I forgot the jug of wine."

That left a loaf of bread and him beside her in the wilderness. She was glad he hadn't brought wine. Resisting temptation was hard enough without the added complication of alcohol. "Wine would put me to sleep," she said, although the opposite was probably true.

He produced some of Kylie's fresh blueberry muffins and a flask of milk. "Yarrawong vintage—" he consulted his watch "—yesterday evening."

"Yesterday was a good day for milk," she said, joining in the joke. After the swim, the cold milk and muffins tasted wonderful, although the company had a lot to do with her enjoyment. She would probably never eat muffins or drink milk again without remembering this moment, she thought, as her gaze was repeatedly drawn back to him. Morning sunlight glinted off his lightly tanned skin. The knotted towel gave him a rakish air, like a latter-day Tarzan in an antipodean jungle. If only they could stay like this for always, keeping the real world and its problems at bay.

His finger skimmed her upper lip, shattering the dream and sending heat spearing all the way to the center of her being. "You would look good with a mustache." His tone was teasing, but there was no mistaking the glint of desire in his eyes.

The reality was a million times more poignant than any fantasy. She swabbed the milk off her mouth and turned away, hardly able to bear the torrent of feelings his touch invoked. "I'll get my clothes."

"What's your hurry?" His arms came around her, and he pulled her against his damp, hard-muscled chest.

She was hot from the mineral springs. Or was it from finding herself in his arms? It was the only place in the world she wanted to be—and the last place she should be. She opened her mouth to tell him how wrong this was, but he silenced her with a kiss that made a mockery of her vow to keep her distance.

He was keeping no such thing, as his lips paid homage to her features, the hollow of her throat and her shoulders, which were bare except for the narrow satin straps of her bra. She should probably end this now but she couldn't bring herself to do it. Only Nicholas could make her feel so sensual, so special...so worshipped.

The car door stood open, and he eased her gently back against the rear seat, the leather cool against her heated skin. Her towel fell away, and his rasped against her legs as he knelt on the seat beside her, all the while caressing her with his eyes.

Now. Tell her you know her secret now, Nicholas's inner voice urged. Tell her it's all right, that nothing matters as long as you can be with her. But as she looked up at him from under half-closed lids, drugged with the passion of his caresses, he couldn't bring himself to break the spell. What if the baby thing wasn't the reason she wanted to leave him? What if she didn't love him as much as he loved her? He didn't think he could stand it if he bared his soul to her and she still insisted she wanted to go.

So he kept quiet and tried to let his touch say what was in his heart. She was the most beautiful woman he had ever known. Not just beautiful on the outside, although he couldn't fault that, but with an inner beauty that years would never fade.

As he knelt beside her, he was enveloped in her womanly scent, which was innocent of cosmetics or perfume yet had a headier effect on him than the costliest fragrance. Cleansed by the mineral lake, her skin felt satiny and still held a glow from the water's warmth. He ran his palm down her side and felt her shudder with pleasure.

Stroking her had ignited fires deep inside him, but he resisted taking her mouth again, wanting to prolong the anticipation for both of them as much as he could. By the time he allowed himself to drink from her lips, he felt like a thirsty man in a desert. She gasped and arched her back, clasping her arms around his neck and murmuring his name against his mouth.

He slid his hands down her back until his fingers brushed the fastening of her bra. Such a flimsy covering for such treasure. It would take no more than a touch to release it, then he could give her as much pleasure as she was giving him and more. It was so tempting that he ground his teeth with the effort of resisting.

This wasn't the way. He cared too much for Bethany to let their first time together take place on the back seat of a Jeep. For her he wanted moonlight, roses, champagne, soft music, candlelight and satin sheets. He wanted to give her the sun and the moon and the stars, take her to heaven and back. And he wanted it "till death did them part."

He still had a few issues to sort out with her, but this wasn't the time and place. They would be resolved as soon as they got back to the homestead. Then when he was certain there was nothing else to come between them, forever could start.

Nevertheless, it took all the self-control he could muster to say, "It's time we were getting back. Your night nurse will need a hand getting her precious charges ready to face the day in their new surroundings."

The timely reminder rocketed Bethany back to earth. She had been perilously close to giving herself to Nicholas, and the abrupt return to reality felt like being showered with icy water. As she looked at him with passion-dulled eyes, she tried to be glad of his strength of will. She wasn't sure she would have been strong enough to end this before it went any further. And it would have been the greatest mistake of her life. This was a fantasy setting; the real world waited for them. Nothing had changed, she thought to herself as she dressed. She was still the wrong woman for him.

But she didn't feel glad. Knowing this was the last time she would feel his strong arms around her and give herself up to the pleasures of his kisses, she felt a dull ache grip her. She was thankful the jolting of the car on the drive home gave her an excuse to wrap her arms protectively around herself. This particular ache would take a long time to heal.

Exhausted by the emotional strain and the demands of the endless night, she let her head drop back against the headrest. She would only close her eyes for a minute....

Chapter Twelve

Bethany was amazed to open her eyes and find Kylie bending over her, a cup of tea in her hand. "Good afternoon."

Disoriented, Bethany sat up. "Afternoon? What time is it?"

"It's lunchtime. It was after six this morning when you and Nicholas got back. You must have been exhausted. You didn't wake up even when he carried you inside."

"Carried me?" The thought of Nicholas carrying her anywhere was enough to set her heart racing. The night's events rushed back—the fire, bringing the babies to Yarrawong and settling them in, the dawn swim at the hot springs and Nicholas taking her into his arms. Her skin flushed as she remembered this last. She had been on fire with wanting him, but he hadn't wanted her.

It was the right decision, although she fought against accepting it. Worn-out with nervous strain, she must have fallen asleep in the car on the way back to the homestead.

Her former room had been taken over as one of the nurseries for the babies, so where was she? The rustle of satin as she moved confirmed her worst fears. She was in Nicholas's own bed, swathed in the black satin sheets that had stirred a host of outrageously erotic fantasies the day she arrived.

"I've brought you some of my clothes, since you had no chance to bring anything with you," Kylie volunteered. "We're about the same size, although I'd give a lot to have your shape."

Kylie had a wonderful figure. The main difference was in Bethany's more generous hips and cleavage. "There's nothing wrong with your shape," Bethany assured her. "It's kind of you to lend me your things."

Kylie shrugged off the thanks. "This is the country. People help each other in a crisis."

"All the same I appreciate it," Bethany repeated. She looked away. "It was good of Nicholas to lend me his room, too." Please let him not have spent the night here, she found herself praying. It was bad enough to be told she had slept through being carried to his bed, without discovering she'd shared it with him, as well.

Kylie grinned, anticipating her concern. "He told me to tell you he slept on the couch in the living room. He's a real gentleman, isn't he?"

"Yes." She couldn't deny it. On the previous occasion when they'd shared a room at the hotel, he had never tried to take advantage of the situation. Maybe he wasn't tempted, she told herself wryly. Just because she became a quivering wreck every time he touched her didn't mean he felt the same way. From his behavior at the hot springs it seemed possible. It was probably just as well, but she couldn't make herself believe it.

She thrust aside the sensuous sheets to find she had slept in her shirt and underwear. Her skirt was folded on a chair near the bed. Had Nicholas...she couldn't bring herself to ask. The thought of him undressing her and putting her to bed invoked such an image of intimacy that her hands shook as she reached for the clothes Kylie had placed on the end of the bed.

At the door Kylie turned. "Nicholas also said to warn you that a couple of reporters are coming to interview you both about the fire. It seems you're quite a heroine."

"Nicholas was the real hero," Bethany insisted. "All I did was follow his lead."

"Its not what the press seem to think. They should be here by the time you finish showering and dressing."

The last thing she wanted to discuss was last night, she thought as she showered, then donned Kylie's peach, short-sleeved T-shirt and checked skirt. The skirt was shorter than she normally wore and the T-shirt felt snug over her fuller shape. But she had little choice. Her own clothes smelled like smoke.

Nicholas's inspection was appreciative when she joined him in the living room. A woman with a notebook balanced on her knee and a man with a camera were already there. The chairs were occupied, so Nicholas made room for her on the couch. She was uncomfortably aware of his knee almost touching hers, the short skirt hitching up to her thighs when she sat down.

"I gather your fiancé was a hero last night," the journalist commented to her.

Bethany shot Nicholas a confused look. But he merely smiled. "Bethany was the real hero. If she hadn't broken the window of the office, the director of the shelter might have died from smoke inhalation."

A lot of things were wrong with his explanation, but the only one that impacted on her befuddled senses was the part about him being her fiancé. She could understand the journalist making such a mistake, but Nicholas seemed in no hurry to correct them.

"I think there's a misunderstanding here," she said.

Nicholas slid his arm around her shoulder. "Don't let my fiancée tell you she isn't a hero or, even more foolishly, try and give me all the credit. She's like that, aren't you, darling?"

Fiancée? Darling? Maybe she was still asleep and dreaming. The journalist beamed at the photographer. "This is a great story. True love and true heroism in one package."

Frustration gnawed at Bethany. "But it isn't…"

"Isn't public knowledge, I know, darling," Nicholas interrupted again. He smiled at the journalist. "Actually our engagement isn't official yet. No one else knows."

He got that right. Bethany felt herself flushing, especially when the journalist added, "Then let us be the first to congratulate you both. I understand you were about to celebrate your engagement when the fire started?"

"Something of the sort," Nicholas agreed. "We were having dinner at a restaurant near the children's shelter when we heard the fire engines and went to see if we could help."

Thankfully the conversation moved on to the fire itself and the details of Stella's rescue. Again Nicholas insisted on giving Bethany an undue amount of credit, but she was too bemused to argue, even though she had done little enough. He was the one who had risked his life to rescue Stella.

She was having too much trouble getting past the part about celebrating their engagement. A chill rippled through her. He had been unusually determined to take her to dinner at the restaurant. Was he about to propose when the fire started? If so, she would have been forced to refuse him, despite every instinct urging her to accept. How could she agree to become his wife, knowing it would mean the end of his plans to have a family of his own?

She forced her attention back to the interview. It seemed that the photographer had been in the area at the time of the fire and had taken a candid shot of Nicholas as he carried Stella to safety. He frowned when they showed him the print. "Just don't make a big deal out of something anyone would have done," he grumbled.

"We plan to use this as the main picture, but we'd also like a shot of the two of you together," the journalist urged. "Can we take one in here?"

Nicholas got to his feet and pulled Bethany up with him. "I have a better idea. Come see what brought the two of us together. Have you heard of a dollhouse called the Frakes Baby House?"

Bethany could hardly believe her ears. Surely he didn't mean to turn the house into front-page news? She had intended to be discreet in her handling of the story, withholding exact details of the house's whereabouts to protect Nicholas's privacy. Now it sounded as if he no longer cared about keeping the house's location quiet.

"Are you sure you know what you're doing?" she asked him in lowered tones as he led the group to the loft above his office.

He misread her concern. "I won't preempt your story. They'll see just enough to whet their appetite for your feature," he promised her. "But I'm doing what my father should have done long ago. It's time the past was laid to rest. After your article appears, I intend to let the house be shown, perhaps at a children's museum, to raise funds for children like those in the shelter." He threw aside the dust cover, revealing the beautiful antique, and turned to the photographer. "You can photograph us in front of this provided you mention that the house will be revealed in full details in the next issue of Bethany's newsletter."

The journalist scribbled frantically while the photographer snapped away, photographing them in different poses, with what Bethany knew would be tantalizing glimpses of the dollhouse behind them.

Finally, the journalist snapped her notebook shut. "What a story. A national treasure turns up on Melbourne's doorstep, tracked down by the determination of one woman, who happens to catch the eye of the house's owner. Then the two of you plunge into a burning building, save the life of its director and provide shelter for five homeless babies. Somebody should make a movie out of this."

Nicholas laughed. "The rights are all yours."

The newspaper people went back inside to take more pictures with the babies in their improvised nursery. The children couldn't be publicly identified, but the photographer wanted general shots of them in their cribs and playing with Georgina and Maree, who seemed to relish her job as junior host.

Watching Nicholas with the children, Bethany felt frozen inside. He acted as if everything the journalist wanted to write was true, when they both knew it wasn't. There was no eternal love story, only a tale destined to end in heartbreak from the moment she had discovered his heart's desire.

But Nicholas was on top of the world as he saw the press people to their car. Bethany would gladly have gone inside, but his hold forced her to maintain the fiction of being his loving fiancée until the visitors drove off down the coach road.

When they were finally out of sight she pulled her hand free. Hurt vibrated in her voice as she demanded, "What are you doing, pretending that we're engaged?"

He looked unrepentant. "You must admit, it makes a great story."

"What happens when the truth comes out?"

He cracked a huge grin. "You have to marry me and make it true."

It was her greatest dream and worst nightmare. She threw herself into a swing seat on the verandah, and it swayed beneath her. "I can't marry you, Nicholas."

He swung himself onto the verandah, and threaded his fingers around the chain supporting the swing. "Why not?"

How could she tell him the truth and face the rejection she was certain would follow? He was so committed to having children that he was bound to change his mind once he knew. Even if by some miracle he still wanted to marry her, she couldn't ask him to make such a sacrifice for her sake. "I can't marry you because...it wouldn't work," she stated.

He stopped the swing and regarded her so intensely that she wondered if he could see all the way to her soul. "Because you can't be the mother of my children, Bethany? Is that the reason why you can't marry me?"

Time stood still. She was glad to be sitting down because her legs wouldn't have supported her at that moment. "How did you know?"

"I've known since yesterday morning when someone at the Southgate Clinic called here to give you some test results. They were all negative. I promised I'd be there to support you when I gave you the news."

"It isn't news to me," she said dully. "Theirs was a second opinion."

"The same as the first?" he anticipated.

She nodded. "Exactly the same. As a teenager, I had a ruptured appendix. It left scar tissue, which makes it impossible for me to have children."

"So that's what the woman meant when she mentioned surgery," he said. "She didn't give it much chance of success."

Bethany shook her head. "The first doctor didn't recommend it, either." She didn't add that Alexander had been the only person to urge her to have the operation. It had been another nail in the coffin of their relationship.

Nicholas surprised her by saying, "You'd need better odds than the clinic quoted to make it worth putting yourself through such an ordeal. Unless it's what you want, of course."

She gave a small shake of her head, her spirits lifting fractionally as she realized Nicholas only supported the surgical option if she wanted it, otherwise he was prepared to agree with the doctors. Then another thought occurred to her. "How did you convince the clinic to give you my test results? They're usually fanatical about privacy."

He grinned. "I told them I was your fiancé. It's becoming a habit."

A habit which couldn't continue. "Even so…"

"I also said we were going overseas as soon as you returned home. Once they knew they were talking to *Dr.* Frakes, they gave me the results right away."

Her eyebrows lifted. "Do you always play so fast and loose with the truth?"

His eyes darkened. "Only when it concerns someone I love. When they started talking about test results, I panicked. I thought you had some illness you hadn't told me about. I thought—" His voice broke and he looked away. "I knew then I couldn't bear to lose you. I came to Melbourne to tell you so."

He gave the swing a slight push, and the motion caused her to reach for the nearest support which happened to be Nicholas's arm. It felt strong enough to support her for the rest of her life if she allowed it. But how could she? He knew her secret and he hadn't rejected her, but he hadn't considered what her situation would mean to his own plans.

He saw the indecision on her face and slid his arm around her waist, drawing her up from the swing into his arms. "I told the reporter the truth. I meant to ask you to marry me, but the fire broke out and I never got the chance. So I'm asking you now. I love you, Bethany Dale. Will you marry me?''

Tears worried the backs of her eyes and she blinked hard. His declaration of love was like a dream come true, but it didn't change the reality. ''I can't,'' she said on a voice that threatened to break. ''You love me now—'' heaven help her, she loved him with every fiber of her being ''—but what about the brothers and sisters you want for Maree? How will you feel when it dawns on you that she'll always be an only child because I can't give you any more?''

His hold tightened, and he pressed his lips to her forehead, then trailed kisses down her nose until he reached her mouth, where he bestowed another gentle kiss before answering. ''You gave me more last night—five of them at last count.''

Her head spun. ''The children from the shelter? They're not available for adoption. Most of them have parents living, but they can't go home because of some family crisis.''

He looked unmoved. ''I know what a children's shelter is for, darling. And I assume all those other rooms at the shelter are usually occupied?''

''Well, yes, but...''

''Then there will always be children in need of the love and care we can provide.'' He kissed her again, lingering this time until her lips parted and allowed him to explore her mouth gently but insistently. Sensuous heat coiled all the way to her toes, and she clung to him, not understanding any of this but lacking the will to put a stop to it. In his present, masterful mood she wasn't sure he would have permitted her to, anyway.

''Nicholas, I—''

He kissed her, silencing her.

''We can't—''

He kissed her again, hard. When he allowed her to come up for air, his eyes shone. "Any more silly arguments, my love?"

She kept silent, getting the message. If she tried to say anything he would only kiss her again. Come to think of it, it wasn't a bad idea. "I don't—"

His lips descended again. Holding the kiss, he swept her down onto the swing seat and leaned across her until the steady beat of his heart merged with her own and his body molded against her. When he finally drew away, she felt as if she had stars in her eyes. She fought the surges of pleasure that threatened to rob her of her last defenses. She had to make him understand. "Please, you must let me say something," she tried as his mouth hovered tantalizingly above her.

"Only if it isn't an objection."

They could go on like this all day. "I don't object to marrying you," she said quickly, before he could start kissing her again. Couldn't he see the heartbreak ahead? "I love you, Nicholas."

He watched her warily. "Why do I get the feeling there's a but coming?"

"Because there is," she said on a deep sigh. "My problem isn't going to go away. What will happen in the future when you regret not being able to have a family like your aunt's? How can I take that dream away from you?"

His delighted gaze roved over her. "We'll still have the dream, my beloved. I didn't understand your problem so it never occurred to me to tell you the whole story about my aunt's wonderful family, which became the model for the one I want." She tensed but he carried on, not releasing his hold on her. "One of my aunt's sons is Vietnamese, two are Aboriginal, and her daughter is Dutch."

Bethany's eyes widened. "You mean they're all adopted?"

"Every one. My aunt couldn't have children, either, but it didn't prevent her from filling her home with children. Most of the time we forget they aren't her flesh and blood."

Thinking of what she had so nearly thrown away, she rested her head against his shoulder. "Oh, Nicholas. Are you sure this is what you want?"

He tilted her face up to his. "*You* are what I want. When I thought you might have some incurable disease it almost killed me, too. I didn't want to live without you. Say you'll marry me, or I'll have to hang myself from the chains of this swing right now."

It was such an absurd idea that she laughed aloud. The swing was at most five feet off the ground and Nicholas was over six feet tall. But she couldn't deny his sincerity, nor the love she heard in his voice and saw shining out of his eyes. "I'll marry you to save your life," she said solemnly as joy and pure physical desire bubbled through every cell in her body.

His look softened and he eased one muscular leg over hers. "You *are* my life. We're perfect together, and as soon as we're married, I intend to show you how perfect."

She groaned aloud. "Must we wait until then?" It would be the sweetest torment she had ever known. She shivered, lost in the ecstasy of belonging, really belonging, in his arms. His kisses made her ache with wanting more, wanting everything he had to give her, and knowing it would be enough for a lifetime.

From inside the house, a baby cried, then was joined by another until a chorus of wails reached their ears. Nicholas grinned wickedly. "It looks like we'll have to."

"We should go in and help Georgina and Kylie," she said, not moving.

"Soon," he agreed. He didn't move, either.

Sometime later he finally allowed her up to tend to their temporary family. But then she was so aroused it was a

miracle she could function at all. Somehow she did. So did
Nicholas, although the caressing looks he kept giving her
didn't help her to keep her mind on the children. Maree
seemed to sense the change in their relationship because
her pleased looks darted between them. Then she held out
her arms to Bethany. "Ma, ma, ma."

Nicholas looked thunderstruck. "Do you think she
knows?"

Then Maree reached for Nicholas. "Da, da, da. Ma, ma,
ma."

His arm came around Bethany, and he linked the fingers
of his other hand with the baby's. "Sounds like you have
Maree's seal of approval. I know you've had mine for a
long time." His lips found hers, and Bethany gave herself
up to his embrace, feeling as if she was finally home.

"Here in this room are all my dreams come true," she
murmured against his mouth.

He shook his head. "Not all your dreams, my darling.
Some things will be strictly between us."

Heat pulsated through her and she pretended shock.
"What do you mean?"

In blatantly arousing terms he proceeded to whisper his
intentions in her ear. If they did even half of what he proposed, they would need a long time, she thought dazedly.
It was just as well he had promised her forever.

* * * * *

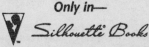

Take 2 bestselling love stories FREE

Plus get a FREE surprise gift!

FIVE STARS
MEAN SUCCESS

**If you see the "5 Star Club" flash on a book,
it means we're introducing you to one of our
most STELLAR authors!**

Every one of our Harlequin and Silhouette
authors who has sold over 5 MILLION BOOKS
has been selected for our "5 Star Club."

We've created the club so you won't miss
any of our bestsellers. So, each month
we'll be highlighting every original book within
Harlequin and Silhouette written by our
bestselling authors.

NOW THERE'S NO WAY ON EARTH OUR STARS WON'T BE SEEN!

OVER
5 MILLION
BOOKS SOLD
SPECIAL OFFER INSIDE

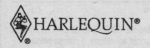

HARLEQUIN®

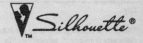

Silhouette®

P5STAR

Silhouette ROMANCE™

COMING NEXT MONTH

#1318 THE GUARDIAN'S BRIDE—Laurie Paige
Virgin Brides

She was beautiful, intelligent—and too young for him! But Colter McKinnon was committed to making sure Belle Glamorgan got properly married. Still, how was he supposed to find her an appropriate husband when all Colter really wanted was to make her *his* bride?

#1319 THE COWBOY, THE BABY AND THE BRIDE-TO-BE—Cara Colter
Fabulous Fathers

Handing over a bouncing baby boy to Turner MacLeod at his Montana ranch was just the adventure Shayla Morrison needed. But once she got a look at the sexy cowboy-turned-temporary-dad, she hoped her next adventure would be marching down the aisle with him!

#1320 WEALTH, POWER AND A PROPER WIFE
Karen Rose Smith
Do You Take This Stranger?

Being the proper wife of rich and powerful Christopher Langston was *almost* the fairy tale she had once dreamed of living. But sweet Jenny was hiding a secret from her wealthy husband—and once revealed, the truth could bring them even closer together…or tear them apart forever.

#1321 HER BEST MAN—Christine Scott
Men!

What was happening to her? One minute Alex Trent was Lindsey Richards's best friend, and the next moment he'd turned into the world's sexiest hunk! Alex now wanted to be more than friends— but could he convince Lindsey to trust the love he wanted to give.

#1322 HONEY OF A HUSBAND—Laura Anthony
Her only love was back in town, and he had Daisy Hightower trembling in her boots. For, if rugged loner Kael Carmody ever learned that her son was also his, there would be a high price to pay…maybe even the price of marriage.

#1323 TRUE LOVE RANCH—Elizabeth Harbison
The last thing Darcy Beckett wanted was to share her inherited ranch with ex-love Joe Tyler for two months. But when Joe and his young son showed up, the sparks started flying. Now Joe's son wants the two months to go on forever…and so does Joe! Can he convince Darcy they are the family she's always wanted?